The Quail

by Dorothy Hamilton

HERALD PRESS
SCOTTDALE
PENNSYLVANIA
1973

To My Father

Garry C. Drumm

The Family

By Frederick M. Hinshaw

Covey of quail explodes with the violence
    and volume of a flight of cousin partridge
    disturbed by the morning stroller
    or roaming dog or fox.

They have roosted on the ground
    in a spot they thought secluded —
    a family or two in the covey,
    twenty to thirty birds protectively colored
    in tan, gray, and white pattern —
    alert heads pointed outward
    on the perimeter.

They fly quickly to cover
    running as they land, then gather again
    to start the day's search for food
    and later, another roosting place.

Seldom solitary the bobwhite quail
    whistles at mating season
    his familiar call, Bobwhite.

When isolated, he finds protection in his color,
    ground cover, and the swift running return
    to his family.

1

Mary Anne Garland stood at the east window of her upstairs bedroom. She looked out over the porch roof and down into the yard. Frost had drained the leaves of the maple tree of chlorophyll, leaving it a giant cluster of red and yellow. A rising wind twirled one reddish leaf through the air. It dipped, turned, then soared upward like a kite without a string.

Music came from Neal's room. She hadn't heard him come upstairs. "He'll be going down again any minute. To run his paper route. And I'd better change my clothes and help Mama. This is her class night."

Mary Anne turned and surveyed her room. It had been her mother's and looked almost the same as when Susan Garland brought her children to Oak Hill from the farm some four years ago. The furniture had been given another coat of white enamel and the knobs were sprayed with gold. Susan and her stepmother had dyed old sheets in soft pink and turquoise and made two braided rugs. One was at the side of the iron bed and the other in front of the chest of drawers.

I love this room and this house, Mary Anne thought as she fastened her pleated green skirt to a hanger with clip clothespins. *So, why have I been thinking about where we used to live all day?*

She hadn't been in the farmhouse out on the Middletown Pike since the day her mother brought them to Grandfather Kirk's house. The only time she'd even seen the place which had been home for nearly twelve years was when they were on the way to see Grandmother Garland for the last time. They took another road to Springvale now.

Mary Anne shook her head as if to clear it of sad pictures as she started downstairs. *Why am I going back — in my mind?* she thought. *Even thinking about living out there makes me gloomy. But that's funny. I don't remember feeling unhappy then. Not often anyway.*

Her mother was standing an awkward distance from the new electric stove. She had to lean over to move the long wooden spoon around in the kettle.

"Afraid you'll spatter yourself?" Mary Anne asked.

"Uh-huh," Susan Garland admitted. "I didn't want to take time to get an apron."

"Oh, Mama! You're always making excuses for not wearing aprons. It's all right if you don't like them. Be yourself."

"I try," her mother said, "and just when I think I've broken the old habit of caring about what others say and do I catch myself doing just that."

"Were you bothered like this when you were my age?"

"Oh, my goodness no," her mother said. "I heard Mama fret about things she heard once in a while. But Papa always teased her out of such moods."

"What's for supper?" Mary Anne asked. "Is there something for me to do?"

"Not much," her mother said. "Everything went well today. This vegetable soup's done. There's baked ham for sandwiches and Apple Brown Betty for dessert."

"Did you do your homework?" Mary Anne asked. "Did you go over your paper for mistakes? Are you sure — "

"I get the point," Susan said. "You're echoing my words. Now that I'm a student again, I can understand how my reminders must sound to you."

Mary Anne took a stack of plates from the end section of the kitchen cabinet, while her mother hurried to the front hall closet and came to the door. "Neal will be back in about an hour and Ellen has gone down to your grandfather's to bring Little Matt home. He's been visiting."

"You look nice, Mama," Mary Anne said.

"Do I?" Susan answered. "I wasn't sure the hem in this jumper was straight. But I didn't have time to ask anyone to check."

"Turn around," Mary Anne said. "It's okay. Or will be when your arms are down."

"Well, I'm going — Oh, I didn't finish. Your father may be a little late. They're sowing wheat today. Keep the soup warm."

"I will. You go on. Or you'll be tardy."

Mary Anne smiled as her mother backed the car out the drive. *She loves being back in school even if it's only two nights a week. Her eyes sparkle more. And she looks younger. Not as old as she did when we lived out in the country.*

As she recalled that time Mary Anne saw something she'd never recoginzed before. *Mama tried so hard to protect us. Never let on when she was unhappy. But I knew — once in a while anyway. At least I did after I was old enough to notice that Papa didn't talk to her much.*

She had her hands full of silverware when the telephone rang. A fork clattered to the floor as she slid the assortment onto a plate.

"Hello," she said.

"Anne?"

"*Yes*, Patty. You should know my voice by now."

"Everyone says you and your mother sound alike. *You* know that."

"Well, maybe." Mary Anne had expected Patty to call. Wishing she wouldn't hadn't helped.

"I saw Roger in the drugstore. He said you turned him down."

"Why do you sound so surprised?" Mary Anne said. "I told you I wouldn't go out with him."

"I don't get it," Patty said. "Any girl in Oak Hill or almost any high school around here'd jump at the chance."

"Let them jump. And why do *you* worry about this?"

"You're my friend. That's why," Patty said. "You stay at home most of the time anymore. You're left out of everything."

"I don't feel left out," Mary Anne said. "Not of anything I really want to do."

"Well, how would you feel if I said Roger asked me

to go on the hayride in your place?"

"It wouldn't make any difference to me," Mary Anne said. "I hate hayrides. You know why, too. And I don't want to go anywhere with Roger. So let's drop the subject. Okay?"

"Okay. See you tomorrow — maybe."

Mary Anne didn't have much time to think about the conversation with Patty or wonder why she'd added the word "maybe." She served food to her brothers and sister, helped Ellen with the dishes, and read two stories to Matthew. His head was bobbing on her shoulder by the time her father came in the back door.

"Dad's home," Matt said as he slid to the floor. "Did you bring any corn for the squirrels?"

"I did," Dirk Garland said as he hung his dusty coat on the hook behind the door. He walked to the sitting room door and said, "Hi, everyone. Having trouble with your lessons?"

"No," Neal said. "Not yet."

"I am," Ellen said. "I don't like these old fractions."

"Well wait until I scrub up and eat a bite and we'll see what we can do."

As Mary Anne dipped steaming soup into the gold-banded bowl she compared her father as he was now to the memories she had in her mind. *It's like he's trying to make up for not paying any attention to us when we were little. For not being at home much of the time.*

"Your mother get off to her class on time?"

"Yes," Mary Anne said. "She had supper all ready though. All I had to do was put it on the table."

"I've told her there's no need to put herself out. We could fix our own food a meal or two a week. Don't you reckon?"

"Sure, Papa. But you know Mama."

"Yes. I do."

Matthew and Ellen had been in bed an hour before Mary Anne went upstairs. She took a library book with her but couldn't get her mind to move with the story. After she'd read the same paragraph three times she gave up and turned off the lamp with the white china shade.

She heard the telephone ring and listened to her father's end of the conversation. *He must be sitting on the stairs. His voice is so clear.* She heard him say, "Sure I think I can spare a few bushels. I always get more seed wheat cleaned than we need."

He sounds tired, Mary Anne thought. *It's probably hard on him to live here and farm over in Eminence Township. Would he rather live in Grandma's big house as he did for a while with Grandpa? Does he ever wish all of us would move? Would Mama now?*

As she pulled a blanket up around her shoulders some of the thoughts of the day went together like pieces of a puzzle. Some parts were missing but she saw a misty picture. *Do my memories of living on the farm have something to do with me not wanting to date anyone? Is that time a kind of shadow? But why? Mama's happy now. And I was then.*

She was almost ready to go to sleep when she saw the sweep of car lights on the wall.

Later she heard bits of conversation from the sitting room which was used for dining when they had company. She didn't try to put the pieces together. It didn't matter what her parents were saying. Hearing their voices was good enough.

2

Mary Anne realized it was raining before she opened her eyes the next morning. Wind was splattering raindrops against the windowpanes. She shivered a little as she pulled the lavender blanket up to her chin. *I have the feeling it's a lot colder outside,* she thought. *I guess it's time. October's nearly here.*

She opened her eyes to the murky light and wondered what time it was. There was no way of telling when sunlight wasn't slanting into the room. She raised up on one elbow and listened to the sounds in different parts of the house. A faint hiss and a few clanks came from the steam radiator along the north wall. *It surely is chilly. Daddy's built a fire in the furnace.*

The wind slapped the wisteria vine against the weatherboarding. The sprays of lavender blossoms were gone but the mat of tendrils would cling to the house all winter and bloom again in the spring. Not even January blizzards could tear it from its place.

I guess I'd better get up. I smell bacon. As she swung her feet to the braided rug she heard footsteps coming up the stairs. *That's Matthew.* She wondered why he was putting both feet on each step before he went on to the next. *He's too old for that. Perhaps it's one of his games.*

Matthew Kirk Garland was the only one of the four children who'd always lived in the square two-story house on the south side of Maple Street. He'd known no other home. He didn't have any memories of the unpainted farmhouse which was situated a half mile north of the village of Springvale. Neither did Ellen who'd been less than a year old the night Susan had brought her children to her father's house.

Mary Anne remembered that she and Neal had been happy when their mother told them they'd be living in Oak Hill. "Mama made it seem right. She said Grandma Garland was sick and Daddy'd have to be with her wherever the doctors said she should go."

Sometimes after her father came to live with them, she wondered why she hadn't guessed her parents were separated, that their marriage nearly ended. *Was it because I was a little kid? I don't think so. Like Mama says, children know a lot more than they ever say. I guess the change didn't upset me because some things were the same. Daddy had always been at Grandma's most of the time anyway. And living here was a lot more fun.*

As she listened to Little Matt's footsteps, thoughts of love flooded her mind, not only for the brother whose eyes were the same blue as her Grandfather Kirk's but for all her family. This sense of love and tenderness included not only her parents, her sister, and her brothers, but also both grandfathers. She was thinking of her daddy's father who lived alone in the big white house out on the farm when Matthew said, "It's past time for you to get up. Mama called you two times already."

"I'm up."

"But you're not downstairs," Matt said.

Mary Anne smiled and asked, "Say, young man, why do you get out of bed so early? You don't have to go to school."

"'Cause I was done sleeping."

"Well, I guess that's a pretty good reason. Is Neal awake?"

"All I know is he's not down," Matt said. "I'm going to see."

Mary Anne felt lucky that no one rang the little bell her mother hung above the bathroom door before she was dressed for school. "Bells sound better to my ears than pounding or yells," Susan had said as she drove the brass nails into the white enameled woodwork. One went in crooked and had to be hammered sideways but the bell held. Sometimes the string which made it jingle had to be replaced.

As Mary Anne buttoned her white blouse she walked down the hall to the boys' room. Neal was sitting at the library table. His dark-rimmed glasses had slipped down on his nose. He looked over the top of the frames as his sister said, "I thought you did your homework last night."

"I did," Neal said. "But I woke up this morning thinking about it. I didn't say enough about the causes of the Civil War in this report. Something on your mind?"

"I should hope so," Mary Anne said. "I'd hate to think it was a complete blank."

"You know what I meant," Neal said. "Are you worried about something?"

It takes a worrier to know one, I guess, Mary Anne thought. *Neal's always been so sensitive and serious.* Then a completely new possibility came to her mind. *Did Neal know Mama and Daddy were really separated? Probably so.*

She shook her head a little as if to clear it of jumbled thoughts. Should she tell Neal how she felt about going out with Roger Trent — or anyone. *He'd understand. But he'd also worry about me.*

"You do have something on your mind," Neal said. "You're standing there trying to decide whether or not to tell me."

"Mind reading again!" Mary Anne said. "Well, you're right. But there isn't time to talk about it now. And it's not urgent. Just growing-up pains I suppose, you could call it."

"We all have them," Neal said.

"Do we? Does *everyone*, I mean some people seem to — to splash happily into this business of leaving childhood."

"I guess you're right," Neal said. "Wonder why we Garlands don't. Hey, look at that clock. We'll talk more about this later. Okay?"

"Okay," Mary Anne said. Somehow she felt relieved rather than condemned for being different from most of the girls her age.

She walked to school part of the way with Ellen, leaving her at the elementary building. Neal rode his bike because he'd promised Granddad Kirk to help put in storm windows that evening. Mary Anne loved walking in the rain. She liked the look of silvery drops hitting small puddles and clinging to telephone wires. *They're shining beads on a long, long bracelet.*

No one came along to join her. Was she early or was everyone else late? *I guess most kids either ride the buses or drive cars or have their parents taxi them.* Several automobiles were either pulling up to the curb or starting away as she turned the corner at the end of the new consolidated high school building.

The mingled scents of wet clothes, rubber boots, a variety of perfumes, and floor polish came to her as she opened one of the four glass doors. And the combined sounds of many differing voices and footsteps filled her ears as she hurried up the ramp to the rows of lockers on the second floor.

She looked for Patty's face among standing groups and moving lines of students. *Probably she's waiting at the locker,* Mary Anne thought. But there was no sign of her friend, then or after she'd stored her raincoat and scarf and loaded her arms with books.

Maybe she didn't come. Sick or something. But she always calls if she's going to be absent.

Patty had been the first Oak Hill girl to come inside the fence and speak to Mary Anne after she came to live in her grandfather's house. Others walked past and looked and one or two said, "Hi" but there weren't many newcomers in Oak Hill then. It took a while for townspeople to include them. It was different now since the furniture factory was built over on the state road. Strangers were common now.

Mary Anne had been glad to find a best friend. She

missed the people in Springvale School and her Sunday school class at Christ Chapel Church. She wrote to a few for a while but as time went on they seemed farther away, more like strangers than people in Oak Hill. The only person she still heard from regularly and saw sometimes was Connie, Rhoda Collins' niece.

Patty and Mary Anne had quarrels but they never lasted long. During these times Susan encouraged her daughter to invite other girls to the house. She did now and then, but always considered Patty her very best friend.

Now as she looked up and down the wide corridor she wondered if her mother was right. *Maybe I do depend on Patty too much. She hurts me a lot. Especially lately. Since she began talking about boys most of the time.*

The warning bell rang signaling only five more minutes until the first class. *I'd better run. I have to ask Mr. Kellams if he approves of my term paper subject.*

Mary Anne was swept along in the stream of her schedule until noon. There wasn't a place to stop and look for Patty or even think about her. She lost her feelings of self-consciousness in the classroom. Learning was a welcome kind of isolation for her. Only she never thought of herself as being walled in. Others were shut out. Her Granddad Kirk called her a born student. He often told his daughter Susan, "This girl will never have to be scolded, bribed, or regimented into studying hard. She's born with a mind open to knowledge. I pray no one, no teacher, shuts its door."

Mary Anne was on the way to the cafeteria when she came face-to-face with Roger Trent. She'd been looking down at her armload of books to be sure she had her assignment notebook. When she glanced up she met the look of Roger's steel-blue eyes. It was a chilling mixture of ridicule and anger. Two of his cronies were on either side, boys who rode the wave of their leader's popularity. Mary Anne dropped her eyes and detoured around the group but not in time to miss seeing the gesture Roger made. He drew an imaginary square in the air.

Warmth flooded Mary Anne's face as she threaded her way around clusters of students. She didn't look for Patty's face, or at anyone's. Halfway to the cafeteria she yielded to the strong impulse to run — to hide. *I'm going home for lunch. I don't know what I'll tell Mama — or what she'll say. But I have to get away from here.*

3

Mary Anne was running before she came to the intersection with Maple Street. She hadn't buckled her raincoat and the corners of the hem slapped against her legs. The sky was clearing and the sidewalk was dry in spots. *I could tell Mama I came home to get another coat when I saw the rain had stopped. But that's pretty flimsy.*

She slowed down as she came within sight of home. Leaving school didn't seem like such a good idea. *I'm like a runner getting caught between bases. I don't know which way to go. But I haven't eaten. And the lunch line is probably closed.*

As soon as Mary Anne opened the door she knew no one was at home. Not because there were no sounds except the ticking of the round-faced clock on the shelf above the radiator, but rather it was a feel, the lack of warmth, of a presence. She hurried through the front living room and the one which had been converted into a study.

She found a note in the usual place under the cut glass vinegar cruet on the kitchen table. "We're helping Nancy paint the bathroom."

We — that means Daddy didn't go to the farm today,

Mary Anne thought. *Too wet to work in the fields.* She was relieved that no one was at home. *I don't have to give an excuse for being here.*

She went to the refrigerator and took cheese, milk, and a bowl of Jello to the table. *A toasted sandwich would taste good but I don't have time for that.* She flipped the switch on the radio before sitting down at the round table. The noon news might blot the hurt of Roger's ridicule from her mind. She thought of calling Patty's home to see if she had gone to school. *But what difference does that make? If she's there, I'll see her in history class. If she's home I don't have time to talk.*

Mary Anne was called to the office at one-fifteen and didn't attend any more classes that day. The student helper said the principal wanted to see her. *I can't imagine why,* she thought as she waited in the outer office until Mr. Davidson finished a long-distance telephone call. *But I haven't been in trouble. So, I'm not scared. Just curious.*

"Come in, Miss Mary Anne Garland," the tall man said as she opened the door which was mostly frosted glass. "Thank you for coming to see me. But I guess you couldn't very well get out of it, could you?"

"Well, sir, I could have run and hidden. But not for long."

"Some try. Some try," the gray-eyed principal said. "Now, to the point. Your records show that you attended Springvale School for five or was it six years?"

"A little over five."

"Do you remember much about going there? Still know any of those students?"

"I remember a lot about the school and the kids too. I see a few of them sometimes."

The principal told Mary Anne the new wing to the Oak Hill building would be ready for occupancy in a few weeks. "Then the full consolidation will be in effect. Since the Springvale building is in the best shape of any of the three county schools it was decided they'd be the last to come in."

"I see," Mary Anne said. But she was still mystified. What did this have to do with her?

"We're having a few problems," Mr. Davidson said. "The people from the other two schools are staying to themselves. In cliques."

"I know."

"You do?"

"Yes, sir. I hear them talk sometimes. Like in the rest rooms, before classes start, or at the lockers."

"They don't like it here?"

"Well — some don't."

"That's natural," the principal said. "It took two elections and a lot of meetings to get the consolidation into effect. But some people are still bitter and students tend to reflect their parents' attitudes."

Mary Anne knew something about the antagonism in the county, mainly from her father. He heard of it at the general store and garage in Springvale. Just before the second election he'd said, "If my mother had lived, and I still lived out there, I probably would have voted against it. Ma hated paying taxes for schools. She'd have fought tooth and toenail against paying for one outside of Eminence Township. And I'd have gone along with her."

"My reason for calling you in is to discuss a plan for breaking down these barriers and overcoming the resentment," the principal said. "Briefly, I'd like to set up a forum, a committee of students — some from the outlying townships, some from here, and a few like you — people who've lived in both districts."

"What would we do?"

"Talk. About problems. Mutual and differing. There'd be two or three faculty members, mostly as observers."

"This might help," Mary Anne said. "I mean if people talked together in a forum they might be more friendly other places."

"That would be one of our goals," Mr. Davidson said. "This school should serve the needs of all its students."

Mary Anne replied quickly and wondered as she talked if she was stepping out of line. "I know one thing that upsets a lot of kids. They have to ride their buses and can't stay for meetings and practices right after school. They feel left out — those who don't have cars or whose parents won't come for them."

"I'm aware of that. Planning along these lines should have been done last year. I jumped at the chance to get this job. But I landed in a puddle of problems. Well, I have to go to the superintendent's office. I'll let you know when this committee is formed. Did you say you'll serve?"

"I will. It sounds like a good idea."

"Fine. Now one more thing. Miss Frances wants you to help her in the library. Your last period is a study hall, isn't it?"

"Yes, and history class is about over."

Mary Anne felt content as she hurried down to the glass-walled library. Roger's ridicule and Patty's absence had faded from her mind. She didn't feel like running from anyone now.

She stayed after school for over an hour after calling her mother for permission. She unpacked a new shipment, putting the cards in the catalog and the books on the shelves. She unwrapped new magazines and lined them up on the racks. *Maybe I'll be a librarian,* she thought. Then she smiled. *When I help Mr. Dane grade papers I think of being a history teacher and last summer when I was a 4-H junior leader I thought of majoring in home economics.*

The sun was almost down by the time Mary Anne left the school building. Only a faint orange rim showed above the fringe of trees beyond the field on the west. *It doesn't seem as cold as it did at noon. Maybe winter's going to hold off for a while.*

Neal came pedaling up from Walnut Street. His canvas paper bag flapped and the tires whirred on the sidewalk. He braked to a stop when he saw Mary Anne. "You're supposed to hurry home," he said. "Mom's taking supper and we're going out to eat with Grandpa Garland."

"Oh! How about you? Your paper route?"

"I only have three to deliver. Granddad Kirk took over some."

"Granddad?"

"Yep. He said he needed to get out of the house. Let fresh air drive the paint fumes out of his lungs. Besides — as he put it — his legs needed limbering."

"Of course you and I both know why he really helped you. He feels sorry for Grandpa Garland — out there alone."

"Sure, I know. But I don't have time to talk. See you."

There probably won't be time to do my homework before we leave, Mary Anne thought as she unlatched the front gate. *Or call Patty or anything.*

Matthew came down the stairs as Mary Anne crossed the front hall. "What's in the sack?" she asked.

"Toys. For Grandpa."

"Does he play with toys?"

"No. Not exactly. But he likes to watch me. You know. He sits and smiles."

"I guess you're right," Mary Anne said as she went to the kitchen. Her mother was taking a casserole from the oven. Milky bubbles came up through a brown crust. "Yummy! Macaroni and cheese. What else?"

"Oatmeal cookies and buttered carrots. And yeast rolls. To be baked when we get to the farm. I called Father Garland. Told him to put a few extra sticks of wood in the range. So the oven would be piping hot when we get there."

"Was he glad to hear we're coming?"

"You know he was. He's so grateful for any good — and uncomplaining about the bad. What kind of a day did you have?"

"Pretty good really," Mary Anne said. "Mr. Davidson

called me in — for a *good* reason. But maybe I'd better tell you on the way to Springvale. I want to change clothes."

"Yes, we should get started. When Neal gets here."

"He's on the way. Where's Daddy?"

"He went out in the truck after the rain stopped."

As Mary Anne changed into blue jeans and a faded red sweat shirt, her farm clothes, she thought of what she'd said to her mother about the day in school. *I didn't mention the bad feeling I had this morning, or confess coming home at noon. And the funny thing is. I didn't even think of it.*

4

"Go a little faster, Mama," Matthew said as they left Oak Hill.

"You in a big hurry?" Mary Anne asked.

"You know why," Neal said. "He wants to see all the animals."

"I'm afraid it'll be too dark," Susan Garland said.

"But the barn has lights in it," Matthew insisted. "I can see the little calves. And Captain. Maybe Grandpa Garland will let me sit on *him*."

Mary Anne remembered how surprised they'd all been the first time they saw the sleek brown Morgan horse. It was on the first Sunday after Grandma Garland's funeral. Daddy was still living on the farm. *Mama thought she ought to offer to cook for them. But none of us kids wanted — the three who were born then — to go in the big house. We never had felt welcome. We didn't know it would be different.*

It was her Grandfather Kirk who suggested they have a picnic. "It's Indian summer and the woods will be a pretty sight. Nancy and I will go along if it will make you feel any easier."

Mary Anne remembered her mother's words. "I

would feel better with you along. I still don't know how, or if, things will work out with Dirk." That was the first time Susan had openly expressed the idea before any of her children that she and her husband were separated.

They rode in Granddad's car that day simply because Susan hadn't taken either the big car or the truck from the farm. Neal had been the first to see the horse. It was tied to the old iron hitching post by the back gate.

Mary Anne remembered how glad her father was to see them. Looking back, it was a sad memory. He came out the back door wearing a clean blue shirt and gray trousers creased like new. His hair glistened, like he'd just washed it. There was a little gray at the sides. *Had it been there before?*

He patted her cheeks, rubbed the top of Neal's head, and put Ellen on his shoulder asking her if she wanted a ride.

"On the horse, Papa?" Mary Anne said.

"No. No. It's not used to little girls."

"Whose is it?" Neal asked.

"It's your Grandpa's. He's always wanted a riding horse. I didn't know it until I saw his face while we were watching a race at the county fair. So, I prodded him into getting Captain. There's no reason not to — not now."

As Mary Anne recalled that day she couldn't remember that her father even touched her mother. He asked how she was feeling and if the walk to the woods would be too much. He bragged on the pressed chicken sandwiches and the hickory nut cake. "This is a lot fancier than our cooking. Right, Pa?"

"That's the truth," Seth Garland said.

Before they left, Grandpa Garland took her and Neal for a ride on Captain holding them with one arm and the lines of the bridle with the other. It was like rocking and floating at the same time.

To Mary Anne, Susan Garland seemed a little happier after that day. She went to Springvale a couple of times and did some cleaning and cooking. Mary Anne began to like going to the big house. No one frowned when she touched the seed picture or put the seashell up to her ear. No one cautioned her to be careful with the stereoptician viewer, or said that she should get permission before she slid the brightly colored cards into the slotted holder. The place began to seem like Granddad's, a house where kids were welcome, and loved.

After Little Matt was born they went more often, when the roads weren't ice-covered or blocked with snow. And after her Papa came to Oak Hill to live with them, they made regular trips to the farm.

Each of the Garland children had their special reason for loving to go to Springvale. *Matt likes the animals,* Mary Anne thought as they turned on to the Middletown Pike. *Neal likes to explore the woods and the creek when the weather is nice. Ellen plays house in the parlor. And I love to curl up in the window seat and read or make up stories in my mind.*

"Look," Susan Garland said as they came within sight of the farmhouse. "Lights are on in almost every room."

"They always are," Ellen answered. "When Grandpa

knows we're coming."

"But it hasn't always been that way," her mother said. "Your Grandmother left every room dark except the one she was in at the time. To save money."

"Was she poor?" Ellen asked.

"In some ways," her mother said. "Even if she didn't lack for money."

"I'm going to the barn first thing. I see a light."

"Be careful," his mother said. "Don't go too close to Captain's heels."

"Mama! He wouldn't hurt me."

"Should I go along?" Mary Anne asked.

"No. Your father or Grandpa are out there or the barn would be dark. You can help me."

To Mary Anne the evening was like a wool coat on a wintry day, or soft covers on a chilly night. She wanted to pull it close, to snuggle in its warmth. Grandpa Garland, as usual, was glad to have them with him. She could remember the years when he seldom spoke, at least when Grandma was around. Now it was as if all the thoughts and stories he'd held back for years were pouring from his mind, like a door had been opened.

His eyes sparkled each time he told of the neighbor who drove his new automobile straight through the back wall. He always ended this story by slapping his knee and saying, "Frank couldn't forget he wasn't driving a horse. He pulled back on the steering wheel and yelled 'whoa' at the top of his voice but the goofy contraption didn't have ears."

Neal often prodded his grandfather to talk about the days when the Indians left Indiana. These tales always ended with the statement, "I wasn't here, you understand. Part of what I've heard may be fancied up a little."

But on this early autumn evening the conversation centered around a subject Mary Anne's father brought up at the table. He hadn't said much before the dessert was served in the crystal dishes shaped like half an apple.

"Pa and I had a long conversation this afternoon. I wonder how the rest of you feel about what's on our mind."

"On your mind," Seth Garland said. "You're the one who did most of the talking."

"Give me three guesses," Mary Anne's mother said. "And I'll not even need two of them. He's trying to get you to move into town."

"Not for good," Dirk Garland said. "Just for the worst of the winter. I know I'd hate to ramble around in this big house alone. To me it's a cold and lonely place in spite of the new furnace."

"It always was for you, wasn't it?" Seth said quietly.

Mary Anne glanced at her mother and saw that her eyes glistened with tears. What kind? Was she happy or sad? *I'll have to ask her later.*

"How do *you* feel about it, Father Garland?" Susan asked. "You've been out here three winters now."

"Well, I tell you. My feelings are six of one and half a dozen of the other. I can't face the idea of leaving the land. But this house was never a home. I reckon you might as well know I've been figuring on something."

He went on to say that he'd been considering the idea of remodeling what they called the Little Barn into a house. "It stands in the little grove up on the knoll. A body can see for miles around on a clear day." He looked first at Susan and then at his son. "What do you folks think?"

Mary Anne's father spoke first. "If that's what you want, then hop to it."

"Susan?" Seth Garland asked.

"I agree. And I can already picture how cozy it could be. Would you make many changes?"

"Some. The walls would be plastered and it would take new floors, of course. And I've always hankered to sit in front of a fireplace. There's enough brick from the old milk house to make one clear across the west end."

Talk of the remodeling filled the evening. The children were as excited as the adults. Neal and Little Matt especially liked the idea of making the hayloft into a bedroom and playroom.

As Susan put the clean dishes away she asked, "Would you let this place stand empty?"

"No. That wasn't my idea. But you may not like what I have in mind. I been talking around up at Springvale. The general feeling is that it wouldn't be any trouble to rent this house. Course I can't help thinking how Bertha would have fretted to think strangers were going to live in her place."

"But she wouldn't have wanted it to run down," Susan said.

"It was always empty, in a way," Dirk Garland said. "Go ahead, Pa. Do what seems right. We're farming the land. Keeping things up. Haven't sold an acre. These things were important to Ma."

"And they are to me too," his father said.

"But you don't need to be a slave to Ma's thinking," Dirk said. "I'll be out tomorrow and we'll go see someone about getting things moving. Now we'd better get these kids to bed."

Stars dotted the sky like golden punctuation marks. Mary Anne leaned her face against the cool window and felt that she was flowing through the night. *I didn't do my homework. I got so interested in Grandpa's little house.* Somehow it didn't seem to matter. School and its problems seemed far away.

Ellen chattered and asked questions until she crawled in bed, then she fell right to sleep. Mary Anne rolled the end of her hair in kid curlers wishing she had some of the jelly-like wave lotion she'd seen at the drugstore. *I'm afraid to use water, it might not dry.*

She wasn't sleepy even though it was nearly ten o'clock, way past her usual bedtime. *Wonder if Mama would let me stay up long enough to read the chapter in the history assignment?* She took her book and walked to the head of the stairs. She saw an arc of light cast by the floor lamp in the living room.

She slipped downstairs and saw her mother reading the Bible. "You studying for something? A meeting? Or Sunday school?"

"No," her mother said. "But I've learned that I rest better when I read a chapter or two the last thing before going to bed."

"You upset about something?" Mary Anne said. "I saw tears in your eyes earlier tonight."

"Not upset. Just touched. Because your Grandfather made it plain that he'd always known how lonely your father was."

"Couldn't he have helped?"

"Not much," Susan said. "He probably tried in little ways. But Bertha — your grandmother — ruled. Everything was hers. She had full ownership — even her son."

"Isn't that slavery? People owning people?"

"Yes. That's the way it always looked to me. But that's enough gloomy talk. That time is past."

But she still remembers bad times, Mary Anne thought. *A kind of cloud comes over her eyes. I used to see that look when I was a little kid. Was she hurt more than she admits? Have her feelings really healed?*

She sat down on the brown leather hassock and faced her mother. "I came to ask you if I could stay up and read my history lesson. Now, I want to tell you something."

"You do?"

"Yes. I think you're — I can't find words good enough. Anyway, I love you."

Susan rested her head on the back of the chair and smiled. "Some feelings can't be put into words, can they? I feel the same way about you. Why don't you go to sleep with pleasant thoughts. Let tomorrow take care of history."

5

As soon as Mary Anne walked in the school building the next morning she saw Patty coming toward her. With an answering wave she hurried down the hall. Then she stopped. Patty hadn't smiled or really looked at her. Roger was walking in the same direction. When he met Patty, they turned and went up the ramp to the second floor together.

"She didn't even know I was around," Mary Anne thought as she went on to the locker area. "Or did she? Anyway, I know now why she hasn't met or called me. I should have guessed."

She told herself that such times were to be expected. She'd seen other friendships dissolve because of boys. *Usually though it's when two girls like the same one. That's certainly not true in this case. I guess the truth is Patty doesn't have time for me if Roger's paying attention to her.*

She felt hurt and wasn't proud of having such feelings. *It's childish and immature. This business of growing up is so — indefinite.* She tried to find a comparison as she went to class. She understood abstract situations and herself better if she could compare them to something concrete. Her Grandfather

Kirk had led her into this way of thinking. To him life was a design and things represented qualities. Grape hyacinths were brave because they came up through the snow of early spring. And killdeers were good mothers because their instincts told them how to protect their little ones.

Mary Anne walked into the classroom before the teacher arrived. She stood at the window and looked out across the fields. Two men were unrolling woven wire fence near a line of green metal posts. The field was being divided by a straight line. *But growing up's not that way. In some ways, like in my grades and some of my thinking, I seem older than most of the girls in my class. But I guess I'm still kind of a baby in other ways. It'd take a crooked fence to mark where I am.*

She took her seat in the second row as people began to file into the room. Carmelita Garzia was the first person who spoke to her. "Where have you been?" Mary Anne asked. "I began to think you'd moved."

"Got used to me? *Sí?*" the girl said.

"Well, yes. After all, no one has ever come between us since I moved here — alphabetically, that is. Or any other way as far as I know."

"No, I guess not," Carmelita said. "It's only the best friends who fight."

Mary Anne looked into the brown eyes of the girl who was still called a migrant even though she'd lived in Oak Hill for nearly seven years. "You sound — bitter — or lonely — or hurt."

"A mixture probably," Carmelita said. "The trucks

pulled out yesterday. The camp is deserted. I go through this every year. I'll get over it. I always do."

The teacher came into the room and rapped for order before Mary Anne could answer Carmelita. But Mary Anne didn't hear much of what Mr. Corbin was saying for several minutes. Had she been unkind to Carmelita? *I know I never said mean things about her or even thought them. But I could have hurt her just the same. By ignoring her, maybe.* She tore a sheet from her notebook, an inch or less at a time, so the ripping of paper wouldn't attract the teacher's attention. She didn't take any notes on Henry David Thoreau until she scribbled, "Wait for me after the bell rings" and passed the message to Carmelita.

In the ten minutes between classes Mary Anne came to know the girl with the coffee-and-cream complexion better than she had in the years of sitting next to her in school. It was like a half-drawn window shade rolled all the way to the top. "Would you like to walk home with me and maybe stop at the drugstore?"

"You don't have to do this," Carmelita said.

"Do what?"

"Be nice to me. Just because I was feeling sorry for myself."

Mary Anne started to say she hadn't given the invitation for that reason. But she knew this wasn't true, not entirely.

"Well, I guess I did ask you for that reason — partly. But there's something else. I'm feeling sorry for myself too." She confided in Carmelita that her close ties with Patty seemed to be stretched to the breaking

38

point. "Do you have a special friend?"

"I don't have much choice, in the winter," Carmelita said. "Only Rosena and Yvonne and I stay up here. And you know girls! When there are best friends, someone is left out a lot. Now I'm the one."

"Does this hurt?"

"No. Not much," Carmelita said. "It used to when I was younger. Now that I'm busy it doesn't really matter."

"You mean busy with school?"

"Yes, and I work evenings. For Mrs. Lyons who keeps foster children."

"I didn't know that," Mary Anne said. "I don't even know a Mrs. Lyons."

"She lives at the edge of town, near the highway."

The class bell echoed through the halls. "I have to go," Mary Anne said. "But could we walk home together part way?"

"Okay," Carmelita agreed.

Mary Anne's mind was busy with school activities until dismissal time. She worked in the library the first half of the noon hour and the cafeteria was nearly deserted when she went to eat. She and Carmelita left by the side door at three-fifteen and bypassed the groups of students who hung around the front entrance when the weather was nice. Neal called them Oak Hill's leisure class. "They don't work or need to. So they fool around!"

Mary Anne had never wanted to be included in the group. But she was a little curious about who was in it and about the fact that it was a mixture of kids who'd always lived in Oak Hill and new ones who came when the factory was built between there and Muncie. What brought them together?

The sun was warm and the light had a tinge of pale silver in it. But the horizon seemed to be veiled in mist. "My Grandfather Kirk calls this kind of weather Indian summer," Mary Anne said.

"What does that mean?" Carmelita asked.

"I know what it means. It's the warm days that come after frost. But I don't know why it's called Indian summer."

"They lived here, didn't they? The Indians?"

"Yes," Mary Anne said. "The Delawares here and the Miamis up north. Maybe others. Were they in Texas too?"

"Yes. But I don't know much about them. I was only nine when we moved. But my papa talks about the Comanches. They crossed the Rio Grande sometimes. On raids."

"You've lived in Oak Hill longer than I have," Mary Anne said.

"I know. I remember when you came. I'd see your mama in the store with all of you. There's so much love in her."

"Yes, there is. But how could you tell?"

"Oh. It shows. In little ways. The way she touched you. The tone of her voice. The look in her eyes."

Tears welled up in Mary Anne's eyes. She looked down at the sidewalk and rubbed one foot back and forth in a crusted patch of fallen leaves. She had to do something until she could talk past the lump in her throat. "That's a beautiful thing for you to say, Carmelita."

"Isn't it true?"

"It's true. It was then and it still is." Then for some reason she couldn't understand, Mary Anne talked about the time when they came to Oak Hill. "Mama was brave. I didn't realize it then. But Little Matt was on the way. And she brought us in to live with Grandpa Kirk. She didn't have any money. I found that out later. And she didn't ask for any from Daddy."

"She must have had a good reason," Carmelita said. "Such a loving lady would not do things because of bad feelings."

"Do you know something! You've put my thoughts into words. Naturally I've wondered a lot about what Mama felt. And I've always known when she was hurt. No matter how brave she acted, her eyes were often — well, clouded like the look of the sky over there."

"I know," Carmelita said. "My mama's eyes hold much sorrow and if I don't hurry home they will show sparks of anger. See you in class!"

Mary Anne felt good as she walked home. "Carmelita has so much understanding. I want to remember what she said about Mama. Someday — maybe — I can tell her. If the time ever comes when she wants to talk to me about what was wrong."

She felt the familiar urge to hurry home to be sheltered. She didn't like being away even for a night. Some of the girls in her class visited each other so often she wondered if they didn't like being at home with their families.

She'd stayed at Patty's three times, but it had always been a bit awkward for a while. Mr. and Mrs.

French were kind to her and to each other. But their ways were different. Their home was like a foreign country. Mary Anne felt like an alien, not because of little things like the Frenches putting gravy only on potatoes and never on bread. There was a more disturbing difference. Patty's parents called her The Brat and teased her — or was it teasing — about always being underfoot and a millstone around their necks. *Mama would never do that, even in fun.*

Mary Anne often wondered if Patty felt unwanted or unloved, but she didn't show any signs of it. She was gay most of the time. The only time she sounded hard was when she said that her parents had parked her with an aunt for the night or a weekend. "So they can be footloose," Patty explained.

The fragrance of spices and tomatoes greeted Mary Anne as she opened the door. *Mama's making catsup,* she thought. She went to the kitchen and saw Nancy, her stepgrandmother, ladling thick red tomato sauce into clear glass jars. "Smells good in here," Mary Anne said. "Where'd you get the tomatoes? I thought frost killed them!"

"It didn't get these," Nancy said. "Your granddad covered the vines two nights in a row. They're still bearing."

"Where's everyone?"

"Well, let's see," Nancy Kirk said. "Your mother and Little Matt went to the grocery store. We're eating together tonight — hamburgers and vegetable soup. Ellen went for her music lesson — "

"And Neal's on his paper route. Where's Grandfather?"

"He went out to the farm. Your father came home at noon and brought Grandpa Garland along to eat with us. They went on to the lumberyard in Muncie. And you know Matthew Kirk! When he heard about the project of doing over the little barn his ears perked up."

"Is he going to help?"

"I think so," Nancy said. "And it's a relief to me. He's not taking retirement well. It's like he's been vaccinated against being idle."

"How about you?" Mary Anne said. "You're not, are you? With tutoring and your painting, you're busy — as busy as before."

"Which is a good way to be. To my way of thinking."

6

The Indian summer lasted nearly ten days. The sun ripened a few tomatoes which were hidden under the tangled mass of vines and Mary Anne found a single rose blooming in the hedge on the south side of the backyard fence.

Her Grandfather Kirk went out to the farm every morning except Sunday. Each evening the children coaxed their mother to go and see how the little barn looked. "We can't go every night," Susan Garland said on Friday morning. "For one thing Papa will be tired whether he admits it or not. And if we take supper and eat out there he'll want to be in on the fun."

"What's the other thing, Mama?" Neal asked.

"The other?"

"You said for one thing. What's the other?"

"Oh," his mother answered. "We have work to do here. Lessons, for example."

As it turned out they made the trip eight out of ten nights and were there from the time church was out on Sunday until dark. Sometimes there was a good reason for going, like taking nails from the hardware store or a couple of sacks of cement.

One evening Susan said, "It's a shame not to take advantage of this lovely weather. Besides, last night's wind probably blew some apples from the Winesap and Baldwin trees."

"And it'd be another shame to let them go to waste, wouldn't it, Mama?" Mary Anne said. "Why don't you admit you're having as much fun as the rest of us seeing the little barn transformed into a home?"

"You're right," Susan said. "But it's more than fun. There's a rightness to what's happening. Like a healing."

Mary Anne wished she could ask some of the questions which had been forming in her mind. But there wasn't time. She had to run to the grocery store for buns for that evening and oatmeal for the next morning, and then go on over and see if Nancy wanted to go with them.

Her grandmother by marriage, was in the side yard digging up canna bulbs. Mary Anne watched as she turned the clump of soil and roots out on the grass. "My goodness, they're ugly," Mary Anne said. "How do such perfect leaves and lovely blossoms come from those knobby things?"

"It's a miracle," Nancy Kirk replied.

"Mama tried to call you. Is your phone out?"

"No. Not that I know of. I'm the one that's been out. Here and down at the superintendent's office. I put my name in for substitute teaching."

"Can retired teachers do that?"

"Yes. But I'm not retired. I just quit a year after your grandfather and I married. I'd taught for so long that I forgot how much time there can be in a day.

Time drags even more since Matthew's been going to the farm."

"But that won't last long."

"No. But he's got his finger in another pie. The carpenter your papa hired says he can use him now and then — as much as he wants to work. But you need to get back and I stand here talking."

"Don't you want to go?"

"I can't," Nancy said. "A mother's bringing her little boy over to get acquainted. He's probably scared and it'll take a lot of patience to convince him that being tutored is not a form of punishment. That takes time."

As Mary Anne hurried home she thought about the real grandmother she'd never seen. *From what Mama says she was a lot different from Nancy. Her pictures show her as being plump with long hair piled up on her head. And Nancy's tiny and wears her hair short and curly. I wonder if Grandfather loves Nancy more or if he misses Mama's mother in some ways. I guess I'm too inquisitive.*

For two days Mary Anne felt comfortable and protected even though she wasn't with her family all the time. She stayed in Oak Hill on Saturday noon and cleaned her room, did her homework, and washed her hair. She didn't even go to the drugstore or the grocery store.

The next morning she woke up wishing she didn't have to go to Sunday school. *What's the matter with me?* she thought as she looked out the window. *I've never even considered missing before. Am I getting to be more like Papa?*

Her father hadn't gone to church with them, not even once, since he came to live in Oak Hill. And she didn't remember that he ever went to Christ's Chapel near Springvale, except the day of Grandmother Garland's funeral.

She sat up in bed and reached for the little basket in which she kept her kid curlers. As she unwound the corkscrews of hair she admitted to herself that she and her father couldn't be staying at home for the same reason. *Roger Trent's not in my Father's Sunday school class.* And she also faced the fact that she wasn't being reasonable in letting Roger make her run and hide all the time. *We live in the same town and go to the same school and church. Besides he misses Sunday school half the time. Maybe this will be one of those days. I hope so!*

Her father was reading the Sunday paper. She saw him when she was halfway downstairs. His feet were propped up on the tan footstool and he wore a white shirt unbuttoned at the neck. *It always seems strange to see him sitting down mornings. He's usually gone or getting ready to go. It was like this even when we lived on the farm.*

Dirk Garland lowered the *Morning Star* and smiled, "Morning, Skeezicks. You're looking mighty pretty this morning. More like your mama every day."

"Well, that's all right with me," Mary Anne said. "This house sure is quiet. Are we the only ones up?"

"No. Ellen and Mama went to cut a bouquet of chrysanthemums to take to church and Matt coaxed

Neal to take him for a bike ride — all the way around two blocks this time."

Mary Anne sat down on the end of the couch. She didn't often get a chance to talk with her father. Now she didn't know what to say but she wasn't uncomfortable around him, and she didn't remember ever feeling that way — not like Neal. Her brother hadn't been happy when their dad came to Oak Hill. He talked to Mary Anne about it the second night. "I've always been scared around Dad. It seems like I never did anything right."

Time and Dirk Garland's changed attitude was gradually making Neal feel easier. At least that's how it seemed to Mary Anne. Her brother talked freely at the table now and he no longer avoided riding in the front seat with his father.

"Everything going all right with you?" Dirk Garland asked. "Your lessons not too hard?"

"No. Not too," Mary Anne said. "Except maybe science. I suppose I'll pass. But I don't like it. It's required or I wouldn't be taking it."

"I reckon we all have some requireds. Some take them. Some do a little detouring."

Mary Anne discarded a sudden impulse to tell her father how she felt about Roger Trent. And about going out with any boy. Girls were supposed to talk such things over with their mothers. *My trouble is I can't mention this to anyone.*

The rest of the day was pleasant for Mary Anne. It was one of the Sundays when the teacher put

"A" for absent after Roger's name in the class record book. During church services Mary Anne thought about the fact that she'd never made good friends with any of the girls in her Sunday school class. *Of course most of them come from outside of town. Almost no one on Maple Street goes to church here, or anywhere that I know of.*

Her mother didn't take a picnic to the farm that day. Instead the whole family, including Grandpa Garland, went to a restaurant in Muncie. "I don't know as I can swallow past the knot in this necktie," Seth Garland said as he climbed into the car.

"It'll do you good to get away from the place a while," Mary Anne's father said. "There is a world beyond the fences of this farm, whether you know it or not."

During the afternoon Susan Garland helped her father-in-law pick out the pieces of furniture he'd want to move. He chose the bird's-eye maple bed and dresser from the room which had been Dirk's, instead of the massive walnut pieces from the other bedrooms. "I'd like to keep the rockers — both of them — to set in front of the fireplace. And the old couch. Its sagging places fit mine. That new set of Bertha's never had any give in it, to make a body comfortable."

"The old one's prettier," Susan said. "I've always loved the deep rose of the coloring. I never understood though why Mother Garland chose it. She liked blue."

"She got a good bargain. That's why," Seth said.

Mary Anne decided to take another look at the little barn. She'd gone out with the others but now she wanted to picture how it would look with the furniture her grandpa was choosing. The fireplace was almost finished. There'd been enough bricks to face all of the west end. The weather had faded them from rust red to soft rose. *It's already like a home*, Mary Anne thought.

She walked outside and sat down near the fence. The sun was still warm and felt good on her face. She heard a rustling from the fencerow. What was there — a field mouse or a rabbit? Or were there some birds which hadn't flown south?

She curled up on the grass which was a little dry and crackly, not green and springy like in early summer. She rested her cheek in her doubled fist and looked down her arm, noticing how the little hairs glistened in the sun. She felt herself drifting into sleep before hearing steps come up the knoll.

"Catnapping?" her father asked.

"Almost. We going now?"

"Not for a while. Your mama and Pa are still fine-combing the house."

Mary Anne watched as her father sat down a few feet away. He didn't speak.

"There," Mary Anne whispered. "I hear something again. Back of us."

Her father turned and looked into the bank of trembling leaves and snowy stems.

"It's a quail," he said.

"I don't see anything that even looks like a bird."

"They don't mean to be seen," her father answered. "They hide where their coloring blends with the foliage."

"Because they're scared of us?"

"Yes," her father said. "Of us and of most everything."

Poor little birds, Mary Anne thought. *Always afraid. That's sad.*

7

It was evening before the Garlands headed toward Oak Hill. They'd been ready to leave when a neighbor stopped by to say that some of the Aberdeen Angus cattle were on the road. "It's that line fence between us and the Collins place," Dirk said. "I knew we should have got a new one built. That old wire's been patched too often."

"I couldn't say until I see," Seth Garland said, "But my guess is those steers have broken off a post. They have been wobbly for years."

"Well, let's get over there before they do damage."

"Want us to go?" Susan asked.

Mary Anne's father started to shake his head. Then he said, "Might be a good thing. You can drive the car. It'll take the rest of us to herd the steers. No need to put them back in that field. Agree, Pa?"

"Yep," his father said. "That fence mending's been put off long enough."

Once the cattle were turned and headed toward the crossroads Mary Anne and Little Matt climbed back in the car. Susan backed up to the Collins lane and turned around. "If Rhoda's seen us she'll be expecting us to come in."

"I don't think anyone's at home," Mary Anne said. "The Sunday paper's still in the tube."

They drove around the square and were stationed at the first of the two four-way crossings before the sleek black cattle came pounding down the gravel road. Turning them wasn't easy. Mary Anne felt that every lowered head was coming straight at her. "Now we'll go south and check them at the next corner," her mother said.

"We're cowboys," Matt said. "In an automobile. Only I'm the only one that's a boy."

By the time the Garlands were within five miles of home Matt was asleep. Mary Anne pulled him closer to her so his head could rest on her arm. Neal didn't say anything but this was not unusual. His silences didn't always disturb Mary Anne. She knew that her older brother didn't do what Little Matt called waste his mouth. She only worried if Neal's lips twitched at the corner during the silent times.

"Somehow I didn't hate to leave Father Garland tonight," Susan said. "He didn't seem as lonely as usual."

"By *usual* do you mean since I moved in town?" Dirk asked.

"No, I don't. Looking back, he's less pathetic than at any time since I've known him."

"You always liked him, didn't you?"

"Yes, I think so. We never talked much. But I always felt he understood me."

They were driving into the last light of the setting sun. The orange red of the sky blinded Mary Anne as she looked toward the windshield. In that light she saw the outline of her father's face as he turned to look at her mother. It was a dark profile against deep gold, like a face on a coin.

"Probably," Dirk Garland said. "You and Pa were sort of in the same boat."

Mary Anne sat on the front steps after she'd offered to help her mother fix supper. "No need," Susan said. "We're only having toasted cheese sandwiches, hot chocolate, and ice cream. I'll let you tidy the kitchen afterward."

Oak Hill was quiet. Someone's radio was on. The melody of "Blest Be the Tie That Binds" came faintly through the duskiness. Someone began to ring the church bell over on Main Street, the only place where Sunday night services were still held. The clangs echoed into each other making a continual sound. They filled Mary Anne's ears and she didn't hear steps on the sidewalk — didn't know anyone was near — until Patty French said, "Hi, Anne!"

As soon as Mary Anne turned her head she wished she'd stayed inside. Roger was with Patty. He didn't speak. He just stood swinging Patty's hand.

"Haven't seen you at school," Patty said. "You been sick or something?"

"No. I've been there."

"Well, I guess I've been too busy to notice," Patty said.

"Probably," Mary Anne said.

"I told Roger when I saw you out here all by your lonesome we really should stop a minute."

Mary Anne wanted to say, "That's bighearted of you to throw a kind word my way. Give me a minute of your time." But she didn't answer, just sat and watched the couple walk away. She heard them laugh. *Probably making fun of me — mopey Mary Anne.*

She leaned her head against the square post and felt a little forsaken. The day had been bright and pleasant and now there was a cloud. "Was that Patty?" her mother asked from the door.

"And Roger Trent."

Susan came out and sat down on the edge of the porch. "Are they going together?"

"I guess."

A dog barked from the backyard of the house next door. It sounded lonely. "Feeling sort of left out?" Susan asked.

"A little."

"This happens."

"Did it to you?" Mary Anne asked.

"Oh, yes. I used to think I was only a between-boys-friend to most of the girls."

"Even to your best friend?"

"Yes, to some degree. I wasn't in a hurry to grow up. In fact, I was scared. And the other girls made fun of me. Felt sorry for me. They never understood why I didn't feel disgraced because I didn't have a date on Saturday night."

"You didn't?"

"No, indeed. I preferred staying home and reading a book."

Is she just trying to make me feel better, Mary Anne wondered. *Or is she wanting to warn me about something?*

"Are the others eating?" Mary Anne asked.

"Yes. But we don't need to hurry in. I can toast our sandwiches later. I want to talk if that's all right with you."

"Go ahead."

"This is not easy," Susan said. "And I don't know why. I've never felt this way before, not with you."

"Have I worried you?"

"Oh, no. I guess the truth is you're so much like me that I'm reliving my hurts in you."

"That's sort of like what Papa said today. That I'm like you. He meant in looks?"

"Is that good? To him?"

"Yes, Mama. Very good."

Somehow Mary Anne knew her mother wasn't ready to talk about what had been wrong in the marriage. She didn't speak at all for what seemed like several minutes. Then she switched the conversation back to the subject of Patty. "I've seen signs that Mrs. French was hurrying Patty into growing up. She says a lot about boys calling." She went on to say that she thought such talk did harm. Other mothers might begin to wonder if their daughters were unpopular.

"Did you wonder about me?"

"Oh, no. In fact I don't like what the word 'popular' seems to mean. It's not always complimentary — according to my values."

Without thinking Mary Anne said, "Roger asked me to go someplace."

"You weren't interested?"

Mary Anne shook her head. "No. But he doesn't take no — he — "

"He's ridiculed you?"

"Yes. Some. Of course I don't see much of him, now that the school's larger."

"Ridicule damages," her mother said. "Especially when it's done because we've stood up for principles."

"But Mama," Mary Anne said. "That's wrong! Or unfair."

"I know. Sometimes I wanted to hit out or strike back. It took years for me to show a Christlike attitude in this."

"I don't understand."

"I read the story of the crucifixion over and over during a bad time. At first all I saw was what you're seeing now — the injustice, the cruelty. Then Jesus' words seemed to stand out. 'Father, forgive them; for they know not what they do.' "

"I don't know," Mary Anne said. "I'm not so sure Patty doesn't know she's hurting me."

"Somehow, I doubt if she does. Some people are insensitive to others' feelings. They don't seem capable of putting themselves in your place."

"Well," Mary Anne said. "I'm getting chilly and a little hungry. Or have you said what you came out here to say?"

"Yes, I think so. I guess I wanted you to know I survived what you're enduring."

"That's some consolation, anyway," Mary Anne said.

Mary Anne tried to concentrate on her homework after she'd eaten and put the kitchen in order. But she was restless. She shut her book and walked to the window. She could see the lighted sign which hung out from the drugstore. *I could call someone. Ask them if they want to go for a sundae or something. But who isn't busy?*

I wonder if Mama would let me go down by myself. I could use some notebook paper. She was lacing her saddle oxfords when Neal came to the door.

"Busy?"

"No," Mary Anne said. "Why?"

"Well, Rob Masters called and asked me down — "

"Who's Rob Masters?"

"The new guy in my class. I told you about him."

"I didn't know his name," Mary Anne said. "Anyway, what does this have to do with whether or not I'm busy?"

"That's what I started to say. They asked you."

"Why me?"

"You sure are full of questions! They have company. Rob's cousin from Ft. Wayne."

"A girl or a boy?"

"A girl. Does that make a difference?"

"Certainly," Mary Anne said. "I'll go."

Lois, Rob's cousin, was a year younger than Mary Anne but the two girls found they shared some likes — accordion-pleated skirts, Hawaiian music, and walking in the snow. By the time Neal was ready to leave, Lois was promising to write and Mary Anne said she'd answer.

"Want to stop by Grandfather's?" Neal asked.

"Will they be up?"

"Sure — I can see the lights."

It was nearly ten by the time they'd reported on the happenings of the day.

Matthew Kirk followed them out. He looked up at the sky. "Stars are out. Looks like good weather for a while. I hope winter holds off until we get Seth's house ready."

"So does he," Mary Anne said. "Good-night."

"Hurry home now," her grandfather said. "So your mama won't worry you're in trouble."

"Where does he think we'd get in trouble in Oak Hill?" Neal asked.

"He didn't think we would. That's just his way of saying good-night."

8

The warm and hazy days of Indian summer lasted for another week. In that time the major part of making the little barn into a home was completed. Mary Anne's father came home long after dark on Thursday evening. The rest of the Garlands had eaten and Susan had left for her night class an hour or more before the truck pulled in the driveway.

Mary Anne hurried downstairs to warm up the chops and take the casserole of escalloped potatoes out of the oven. As her father began to eat she chopped lettuce and diced carrots into an individual salad bowl. She listened as he told her about the plans for Saturday and Sunday.

"The little barn is about ready. The fireplace is finished. The floor laid and the plumbing done. Just a few finishing touches and your grandpa can move in."

"Like what?"

"Putting another coat of varnish on the floor. And Pa's bound to get a grate and screen for that fireplace. I never saw him so set on anything."

"He's probably thought about it for a long time," Mary Anne said. "Wanted it a lot."

Her father clinked his fork against the edge of his plate several times before he spoke. "Like your mama wanted to finish college."

Mary Anne pulled out a chair and sat down on the opposite side of the table. The light from the brass hanging lamp included both of them in its circle. "I never knew Mama wanted to finish college. That it was real important to her, I mean. She never said much about it."

"No. And for a good reason," Dirk Garland said. He rubbed the heel of his hand back and forth across his forehead.

He only does that when he's worried or upset, Mary Anne thought. *Why, what went on between them that I don't know?*

"I was against it," Dirk went on. "Thinking women didn't need education for what they were put on earth to do, I told her. I'm ashamed now at what I said. I was about as wrong as a person could be."

Mary Anne didn't know what to say. She'd learned more from this statement about the trouble between her parents than she'd ever known. Should she ask questions? Would her father say more? She got up and went to the refrigerator. As she scooped ice cream into a cut-glass dish, her father turned back to the subject on which he'd opened the conversation.

"Pa's coming to Oak Hill in the morning and pick up your other grandpa — after he puts on that coat of varnish. They're going into Muncie to pick out the fireplace fixings. I told him to get what he wants, no matter what it costs. He can afford it. And if he's not earned the right I don't know who has."

"How's Grandpa Garland going to get here?" Mary Anne asked.

"In the car."

"I never saw him drive," Mary Anne said. "He always walked when he came to see us on the farm. And you bring him here. I thought he never learned."

"I can see how you'd get that idea," Dirk Garland said. "He didn't drive much for two reasons. The cars and trucks were Ma's. And your grandpa was content to stay at home — or on the land."

"Does he want any help moving?" Mary Anne asked. "Like from us?"

"He's counting on that. Wants us to make a day of it."

As Mary Anne rolled her hair up on the banana-shaped curlers, she thought of Patty. *Last year or even last month I'd have called and asked her to go with us Saturday. And she'd probably have gone. But not now. She wouldn't get that far away from Roger.*

She shook her head. *I don't want to think about that, or them, anymore. What they do and say isn't bothering me as much as it did. I'd be better off if they leave me alone and I can manage to stay out of their way.*

Mary Anne was a little later than usual getting to school the next morning. Not being ten minutes early was almost the same as being tardy for her. As she picked up her books her mother asked, "Could I put another one on that stack? Do you have time to take it to Nancy?"

"Sure. What is it?"

"A book about helping the disadvantaged child. I got it for her at the library last night."

"She's trying to solve another problem."

"Yes, and she probably will."

Nancy and Mary Anne's grandfather were eating breakfast. "Grab a muffin," Matthew Kirk said. "They've got blueberries in them."

"They smell yummy but I have to run. Thanks anyway."

"Go ahead. You're likely to be only five minutes early. Break your record."

Mary Anne smiled and wrinkled her nose at her grandfather. She knew he was only teasing, that she had his wholehearted approval. *That kind of teasing I can take. You know what it is.*

As soon as she walked through the door of the school building she became the victim of bantering. Roger Trent and three or four other boys were standing near a water fountain. Mary Anne glanced that way and started to walk in the opposite direction. *I can go up the ramp and then down to the lockers at the other end of the hall.* But she didn't move quickly enough to avoid hearing what Roger said. "Well if it isn't Miss High and Mighty. You guys know her. The mama's girl of Oak Hill."

Mary Anne felt as if her feet were nailed to the floor. She stood at the foot of the ramp wanting to run but couldn't move. Roger kept on shouting taunts at his target. "You guys know Annie, don't you, or does she even let you get that close?"

Something, a surge of courage, or a dash of defiance, came to Mary Anne's mind. She turned and took the direct route to the lockers. As she was even with the group she stopped and faced them. Her cheeks were burning, her mouth was dry, and her books clenched against her chest. She didn't look at Roger. Instead her eyes focused on Clay Gilbert. She noticed that he looked as uncomfortable as she felt. There was a white line around his mouth and he rubbed one hand up and down on his thigh. "They know me now, Roger. You just introduced us."

She felt relieved as she walked away. *At least I didn't run or cry. And what did he say that was so shameful? Roger'd call any girl high and mighty if she turned him down. And I don't see anything wrong about being a mama's girl. Of course, Roger probably does. But I don't have time to think about what's in his mind.*

She ate lunch with Carmelita that day. The meeting wasn't planned. They reached the cafeteria door at the same time. "I don't remember ever seeing you here before," Mary Anne said.

"For a good reason. I always go home. But today I'm rushed for time. A report's due tomorrow. So I'm off to the library after I grab a bite or two."

"Will you sit with me if I promise not to talk too much?"

"Sure," Carmelita said. "Talk all you want. But I warn you. When it's time to go, I'll leave."

"Well, mainly I've wondered about your baby-sitting, with the foster children. Do you like it?"

"Oh, *si*," Carmelita said. "There I go! When I'm really excited about something I revert to Spanish. Or when I'm angry." She went on to say that she looked forward to going to the big house on the edge of the highway. "Sometimes I feel sad. But it's really *bueno* to see how many hurts loving care can heal. Now I must go. See you."

Mary Anne was finishing the chocolate pudding when someone pulled out the chair across from her. It scraped on the green tiles of the floor. She glanced up and saw Clay. He sat down and looked straight into her eyes. "I'm sorry, Mary Anne."

"For what? You didn't do anything."

"That's just it! I should've done something. Spoken up, or walked away, or socked Roger in the nose — or his big mouth."

Mary Anne smiled. "Now, Clay! You know you'd never hit anyone in your whole life."

"You're right. I've got the courage of a rabbit — a medium-sized one."

The image of the brown and white quail came to Mary Anne's mind. For an instant she saw it, shrinking into the protective coloring of the leaves. "Don't be hard on yourself, Clay. It wouldn't have done any good to stick up for me. You'd have only prodded Roger into saying more."

"Maybe," Clay said. "But I just wanted to tell you I know what's itching him."

"You do?"

"Sure. You turned him down. He conducts a real hate campaign against girls who say no to him."

"How many is *all*? Who besides me?"

"More than you might realize," Clay said. Then he smiled and added, "You didn't think you were the only sensible girl in Oak Hill High, did you?"

"Thanks," Mary Anne said. "I guess that was a compliment."

"It was. And you're welcome. I have to run or I'll miss the bus. My science class is going to Ball State University this afternoon."

As Mary Anne carried her tray toward the counter she wondered, *Would Clay have told me why Roger called me a mama's girl or does he even know? Is that a way of saying I'm a big baby or does he mean something more insulting? I guess I'll not ask. Maybe I'm better off not knowing.*

She stopped at the post office on the way home. Once in a while her mother didn't walk up for the mail. She saw two letters through the glass door of Box 327. One was for Neal. *He's probably been answering ads again.*

The other was addressed to her and was from Lois, the girl she'd met at Robin Masters' home. Mary Anne read the two pages as she walked home. "We've moved since I was in Oak Hill, out of the city. I go to Southport High now." The letter told Mary Anne much that she hadn't learned in the one visit, about Lois' family, her church activities, and her work as a candy striper in a hospital.

Lois closed by writing, "I told Mother about you and she suggested that you come here for a visit during the teachers' association vacation. My aunt's bringing Rob and I'm sure you can hitch a ride. Let me know soon."

That sounds like fun, Mary Anne thought. *I'll ask Mama as soon as I get home. I'm sure she'll let me go. But knowing her she'll probably check with Mrs. Masters and write to Lois' mother. She never wants any of us to be where we're not welcome.*

9

Before Mary Anne went to sleep that night she relived the conversation with Clay Gilbert. Somehow he'd erased some of her loneliness of feeling left out at school. Having even one person respect her for what she was canceled the disapproval of several. *How can that be? Is good always stronger than wrong?*

She fluffed her feather-filled pillow, turned over, and looked out the window. The moon was full, not a tissue-paper circle of pale gold or a platter of misty silver, but an orange ball. The words of "Shine on Harvest Moon" came to her. *That's one of Grandfather Kirk's records. I haven't heard it for a long time.*

That thought led into the trip both her grandfathers had made that morning. She'd heard about it at suppertime. "I don't know who got the biggest kick out of it, Pa or Matthew," Dirk said as he sat down at the table. "I doubt if either swallowed more than a half-dozen bites of the chili and fruit salad you fixed, Susan. They couldn't wait to get the grate in place and build a fire."

"A real for sure fire?" Little Matt asked.

"A crackling, sparking fire," his father answered.

"The chimney has a good draw on it. You could almost hear the smoke going up."

"Can you hear smoke?" the little boy asked.

"No. I reckon not," his father said. "I probably imagined that."

Mary Anne remembered that her father had shaken his head and said, "I'm pretty slow at learning that a person'd better watch what they say to kids — keep it straight."

I know what he means, Mary Anne thought. *He wasn't at home much when Neal and I were little. And didn't talk very often then. Is that why he puts down his paper when any of us say anything and hunts us up when he comes home from the farm?*

The thought of the farm led to other unanswered questions. *Will we ever move out to the big house? Does Papa want that? Or do I?* She shivered a little and pulled the blanket up over her shoulder. *I don't think Grandma Garland's house will ever seem like home and I don't want to even think about leaving here.*

That reminded her of what her mother had said about the visit to Indianapolis. *Almost word for word as I expected. She'll talk to Mrs. Masters either tonight or in the morning. But I know she's in favor of my going. How did she put it? "It's always good to push back horizons a little. Otherwise, they tend to close in."*

Mary Anne raised up on one elbow, turned on the lamp, and looked at the round-faced clock. *Nearly eleven! I've got to stop this chain of thinking. Not let this last link hook on to another.*

She closed her eyes and concentrated on the words of the Twenty-third Psalm. Drowsiness began to overtake her on the sentence, *He leadeth me beside the still waters,* and overtook her as she thought, *My — cup — runneth — over — .*

She wasn't sure what wakened her the next morning because sounds were coming from both floors. Her father was in the front hall talking on the telephone. She heard him say, "Do you want to ride out with the boys and me? Or come with the ladies? Okay, we'll be past in — say fifteen minutes."

Mary Anne stretched her arms back and above her head and blinked at the morning light. *I'd better get up or I'll be left behind. And Mama probably could use a little help.* She met Little Matt on the stairs. "Where you going?" she asked. "I thought you'd be out in the truck waiting."

"I was. But I forgot my present."

"What present? Did you buy Grandpa another toy?"

"No. I got him something for his house. But you can't see it. It's a surprise."

"I see," Mary Anne said as she chucked her little brother under the chin. She could tell he didn't always like being patted. He was getting bigger, as he kept reminding her. But reaching out to touch him was a part of her nature. All of them, her mother and grandfather and even little Ellen, had poured love on the baby born after Susan brought her children to her father's house. It was like they all needed to love one another and someone in common.

"Hello, Skeezicks," Mary Anne's father said as she walked into the kitchen. "We were wondering if we

70

were going to have to call you."

"She's a sleepyhead," Ellen said. "I beat her up."

"For the first morning in a long time," Mary Anne answered. "Besides, you don't look so wide awake yourself."

"Susan," Dirk Garland said, "aren't you going to sit down? You've been on the go — I don't know how long."

"Well, it didn't seem smart to sit down when I have to keep jumping up to take cookies out of the oven."

"Cookies," Mary Anne said. "You baking today?"

"You know me," her mother said. "At the last minute I get afraid we're not going to have enough to eat. But I should have thought of something less time-consuming."

"Here, I'll take over," Mary Anne said. "You eat."

It was nearly nine o'clock before the dishes were washed, the picnic basket packed, and they pulled up in front of Grandfather Kirk's house. Nancy came down the steps carrying a brown paper bag. "You didn't need to bring food," Susan said.

"I know," her stepmother answered. "But I went to the fruit market in Muncie yesterday and yielded to temptation. Tokay grapes and Bartlett pears have that effect on me."

Moving three rooms of furniture wasn't enough work to fill a whole day and occupy nine people. There was time for much laughter and conversation and a long lunch hour. They ate under the maple trees at the side of the little barn. "I sort of figured on having a sit-down meal inside but I guess I got the cart and horse separated. The tables are moved but not the dishes."

"We don't need dishes for what's in this basket," Susan said. "And we can eat inside when the weather's bad. In front of your fire."

"I did a little deliberating about lighting the first log," Seth Garland said. "I had me a choice. To have my folks here when I touched the match to the shavings and kindlings. Or have the blaze welcome all of you."

Mary Anne glanced at her mother. She was unfolding the damp towel from the stack of foil-wrapped sandwiches. Her eyes were misty. *She knows how important this day is to Grandpa. Maybe better than any of us. I wonder why?*

By early evening all the furniture was in place, the rocking chairs at either side of the fireplace and the soft couch on the facing wall. Susan and Nancy had spread the bird's-eye maple bed with crisp sheets, a plaid blanket, and a patchwork quilt which was one of the few things Seth had brought to the big house. His mother had made it.

"I never saw this, Father Garland," Susan said, when he brought it to her wrapped in crackling brown paper. "Of course there are probably a lot of Bertha's things I've not seen. I wasn't in the house much."

"Neither was this quilt," Seth said. "It's been in my old trunk in the hayloft, almost from the time I came here."

"It's beautiful," Nancy said. "Jacob's ladder pattern. And it's not yellowed with age. That's surprising."

"Well, I sort of saw to that," Seth said. "I took it over to Rhoda Collins now and then. To have it done up."

"I'd gladly have washed it," Susan said.

"Don't you reckon I know that?" Seth said. "But I figured you had your clotheslines as full as you needed."

Mary Anne glanced at her father. He was standing in the doorway with a load of short logs in his arms. *He looks so sad. Like what Grandpa just said is painful.* Little Matt changed the subject when he came to the head of the ladder which led to the upstairs loft. "You guys about done down there?"

"I think so," his mother said. "Why? You're not wanting to go home, are you?"

"No," Matt said. "I've got a present for Grandpa's house. When you're all done I'm going to give it to him."

"That's right," Susan said. "I forgot."

"You know about this? What is it?" Mary Anne whispered.

"I know. He couldn't quite manage alone."

"Everybody sit down," Matthew said. "While I go out to the truck."

"He's feeling real important," Neal said as he pulled a cane-seated chair out from the end of the drop leaf table.

"That's everybody's right," Seth said. "At least now and then."

Matt came back with a paper shopping bag bumping against his legs. He walked up to his grandpa who was sitting in the rocking chair with the highest back. "Here," the little boy said. "This is for when I come to stay all night."

Everyone watched as Mr. Garland pulled a black tin

corn popper from the bag. "See," Matt said. "It's got two handles. This one fastens on. It'll reach all the way into the fireplace — from way back."

"Well now. I don't know as I ever could have thought of a better present than this," Seth said. "When do you reckon we could try it out?"

"Tonight maybe," Matthew said. "That's why I bought some popcorn. With my own money."

"I don't know of a better time," Seth said.

"Are you sure you want to stay all night?" Susan asked. "You never have."

"Well, I'm big enough now," Matt said. "If Neal stays too."

Mary Anne looked around the room. Everyone was smiling. Tenderness showed on every face, especially Neal's. *He feels good*, she thought, *because Little Matt wants him along. He doesn't let his feelings show much. Not in words anyway. But he can't hide that look.*

"I didn't bring any extra clothes," Susan said. "Those show you two have been working."

"I can bring some back out," Mary Anne's father said. "Besides, I came off without the two blocks of salt for the cattle. They're about out."

He's just making excuses, Mary Anne thought. *To make it easy for the boys to stay.* She rode back to Oak Hill in the truck. Neither she nor her father said much until they were halfway home. "I thought maybe Mrs. Collins would be over today," she said.

"Didn't you hear?" her father answered. "She's coming tomorrow. A few of the neighbors are having a housewarming."

"Does Grandpa know?"

"Yes. Rhoda talked it over with him. Wanted to know who he'd like her to invite. Who he'd enjoy seeing." As they came within sight of Oak Hill he said, "You like Mrs. Collins, don't you?"

"Oh, yes, Papa. I remember so many nice things about her and being at her house. I loved to play in the grape arbor. It was like a little greenhouse. And after I started to school she loaned me books. Her house was like a library to me — and to Mama and even Neal. He learned to read at Springvale."

Her father reached over and rubbed one forefinger up and down on the back of her hand. "I'm glad Rhoda gave you some good times. You and your mama."

10

The Indian summer ended the next day. The thin haze, which had silvered the sunshine for a week and a half, was a heavy fog that Sunday morning. As Mary Anne walked downstairs she heard a weather report coming from the radio in the kitchen. A cold front was moving down from Canada and the temperature was expected to fall below freezing.

Her mother was alone in the kitchen. "Are we the only ones up?"

"No," Susan said. "Not quite. Your papa is in the garden. He heard the heavy frost warning earlier and is bringing in what won't stand a hard freeze, tomatoes and green lima beans."

"Sounds like winter's near," Mary Anne said.

"Yes. But it's time. And I guess we're prepared."

"You sound like it's one of your favorite times."

Her mother had been slicing stacked strips of egg noodle dough. The serrated knife made hoarse sounds as it hit the cutting board. She stopped and ran the tip of her tongue back and forth on her lower lip. "The truth is, my feelings about winter are as changeable as Indiana weather. I loved it when I lived here as a child. Not as much when we lived on the farm.

But now it's good again."

She went on talking as she resumed work. The coughing of the brown-handled knife punctuated her sentences.

She reached back into what she called her bank of memories and brought out bright moments from her childhood. After the first hard frost their family had hot cocoa every evening before bedtime. Her mother brought it to the living room, which was called a parlor then, in tall cups which had been *her* mother's. "They weren't thick and durable. They were of china so thin you could almost see through them when you held them up to the light. The rims were flared and a spray of gold leaves circled the top.

"I've seen them, you know," Mary Anne said. "On the top shelf of the china cupboard."

"Yes. They've been there since Mama fell from the ladder under the cherry tree. Never used. I've washed them during housecleaning. And that's all."

"What else did you do for fun in the winter?" Mary Anne asked.

"Maybe nothing which would seem unusual to you. Papa and I took long walks in the snow. This was more fun right after it fell. We made our own path — didn't walk in the steps of others. Papa knew the tracks of every animal and bird. And we made snow ice cream."

"So did we," Mary Anne said. "You always said the same thing. 'Don't dig down too far to where it's dirty.'"

"I know," Susan answered. "That's what my mother told me."

"You said we'd get sore throat if we ate too much. But we never did."

"Neither did I."

Mary Anne looked at the clock. "I guess I'd better get ready for church. Before there's a rush for the bathroom."

For some reason the mention of church made her think of Rhoda Collins. Was it because she remembered riding to Christ Chapel with the neighbor who lived on the road west of Springvale?

"Mama, do you know something! We haven't seen Mrs. Collins for a long time."

"I realize that," Susan said. "I've made a resolution to take a day — this week — and go out there. It's not right to get so busy there's no time for special people. It's typical of her to be doing what's in store for your grandpa today. So like her."

"I know about that," Mary Anne said. "Papa told me. There's one thing I don't understand. Why weren't we invited?"

"We were."

"Papa didn't say so."

"He doesn't know," Susan said. She glanced toward the back door as she sifted a dusting of flour over the mound of noodles. "Rhoda called me and I decided not to tell him. It's best that we not go. It's hard for me to put this into words, honey. But coming to live here was a giant step for your father. He had to overcome a lot of pride and self-will and the lingering influence of his mother."

"Didn't he want to come?"

"Oh, yes. That's just it. He had to want to be here

very much in order to — well, there's only one way to say this — in order to admit he'd been wrong."

"But what does this have to do with today — with you not telling him?"

"This," Susan said. "He can swallow the feelings when he's with us and a few others. But most of the people who are going to the little barn are from Christ Chapel Church. Your papa hasn't risen above the prejudice against churches. That's part of his inheritance, I guess. And he's still not comfortable around people who've known me all my life. I see why."

"You understand a lot," Mary Anne said.

"I should," her mother answered. "And in a way that's been a kind of salvation. Knowing why people do things is like an ointment. It soothes the pain."

"You sound like Grandfather Kirk. He's always comparing things to feelings."

"That's natural," her mother said. "And a compliment, for which I thank you."

Mary Anne felt good as she went upstairs. Whatever had been wrong in her home, things were better now. "But I still wish I knew more. I'm not as strong as Mama. I just know she's been hurt deep down. I couldn't bear much. Look how upset I've been because of Patty and Roger."

The warm feeling which had been sparked by the conversation in the kitchen lasted all day. The temperature outside began to drop about noon, but she felt as if the Garlands were covered by a blanket of warmth and security. They enjoyed Ellen's "very most favorite meal," of golden egg noodles, buttery mashed potatoes, and creamed green limas.

"You don't have to say 'very' and 'most,' " Neal said as he put strawberry jam on a crusty biscuit. "Favorite means best."

"Oh, Neal," Ellen said. "You're the one that talks like a dictionary. I just plain talk."

Dirk Garland smiled and patted Ellen's shoulder. "You go right ahead. Be yourself. But give your brother the same right."

Mary Anne saw a flush in her older brother's cheeks. *He's pleased,* she thought. *Papa made him feel good.*

The telephone rang as they were eating.

"May I answer," Ellen asked.

"Yes," her mother said. "But listen closely. Be sure you understand who's calling and who they want."

After a couple of minutes Ellen turned and said, "It's Grandfather Kirk. And he wants all of us to go to the apple orchard, down by New Castle."

"Who's in favor?" Susan asked.

Mary Anne raised her hand and looked at everyone. No one voted no, not even her father.

The car and the afternoon were crowded. The trip included a stop in Memorial Park. Matthew Kirk took Little Matt for a walk along one of the wooded trails. "Now the rest of you are welcome to tag along," he said. "But Matt's the only one who's the right size to have the proper viewpoint."

"What do you mean?" Nancy asked.

"It's simple. From where you and I stand, a walk through the shrubs and undergrowth might be a kind of bothersome experience. We'd be brushing branches back to keep from getting scratched. But to a person Matt's size they're like trees are to us. He's got a different perspective. His view will be clear. The path ahead will be plain to be seen."

"But Grandpa," Neal said. "You're tall. You'll be up above Matt."

"Not in my mind. I'll be right where the boy is. There's the place where the trail begins."

"That man," Nancy said as the tall man and the boy who was not quite five started up the wooden steps which led to the head of the trail. "He never ceases to amaze me. He has a mind that spans generations."

"And a soul which includes all of them," Susan added.

"You know," Dirk Garland said. "In a lot of ways he and my pa are alike, which surprises me. Pa never went past the eighth grade. And Matthew went to college and taught school a long time. But they sure hit it off. You should hear them talk while they work. It's like a book."

"It's shared wisdom, Dirk," Nancy said. "The kind that doesn't necessarily come from books. Not that good ones don't offer a lot."

Mary Anne and Neal walked all around the lake while their father took Ellen up the hill to see the Civil War cannon. Nancy and Susan sat on a slatted green bench and talked as they watched the white and mallard ducks and the crook-necked swans sail on the breeze-ruffled water.

It was after three o'clock before they drove down the graveled lane which led to the apple orchard. They were there over an hour and Mary Anne wished they could have stayed longer. This time she was the one who went walking with her grandfather. No one else seemed to be interested in wandering along between the rows of trees.

Picking had started but many limbs were still bent by the weight of their fruit. Tall ladders leaned against a few trees. A loaded wagon stood at the end of one row. "They're Winesaps," Matthew Kirk said. "Probably windfalls. See, some are bruised. They'll be used for making cider in a day or so."

"Do you know the names of all the apples in this orchard?" Mary Anne asked.

"Possibly," her grandfather said. "If I don't, this would be a good opportunity to find out where my ignorant spots are."

They walked slowly stopping at each tree, while Mr. Kirk looked at the fruit, and touched or smelled it. Mary Anne heard the names, Rambo, Wolf River, Jonathan, Maiden Blush, Yellow Bellflower, Red Delicious, Baldwin, Ben Davis, Grimes Golden, and Fall Pippins. "They're like poems, Grandfather," she said. "Even the names are — delicious."

"Maybe your senses are being influenced by your thinking. The aroma of this place is heady."

Once in a while they came to a tree without apples. "These are early varieties," Matthew said. "Yellow Transparent maybe or early Junes."

"How do you know all those names? Was this something you learned in college?"

"No. We had an orchard at home. Most farms did then."

They were nearly at the end of the last row when Matthew stopped and looked puzzled. He picked up a fallen apple, turned it around in his hand, and sniffed. "I never saw this one before." He took the pink-cheeked fruit with him to the low building which was both a salesroom and storage shed. A tall man in striped coveralls came to meet them. "What's the name of this apple?" Mr. Kirk asked.

"That's a Colonel Matthews," the orchard owner said. "A good all-round fruit."

"It's bound to be," Mary Anne's grandfather said as he grinned at her. "It's bound to be, with a name like that."

11

It was nearly five o'clock before the Kirks took their peck of apples and half gallon of amber cider out of the car, and waved good-bye to the Garlands. The sky was a dome of dark gray and an east wind blew leaves down Maple Street. They skittered and danced and some had been crushed under tires.

Little Matt, on his knees, looked out the back window as they headed toward home. "Grandpa didn't get a bunch of apples like we did. Was he about out of money?"

"I think he got all he wanted," Susan said. "Remember there are three times as many of us."

"Three times!" Matt said. "I guess we're a pretty big family."

"A family who likes apples anyway," Dirk said.

"The house may be a little chilly around the edges," Susan said. "It's surely a lot colder than when we left."

"Didn't you hear me building a fire," Mary Anne's father said. "I figure none of you will have to stand around with your coats on."

"I think I'll go on upstairs, Mama," Mary Anne said. "Unless I can help do something."

"No. This will be a leftover meal. We've all had apples and a glass or two of cider. No one should be very hungry."

"I was wondering," Dirk said. "If you'd mind putting supper off for an hour or so. We're selling some steers tomorrow. And if I don't get out there, Pa may take it in his head to sort them by himself. They're not the tamest animals in this neck of the woods."

"Go ahead," Susan said.

"Anyone want — " Then Dirk stopped. "Or should I ask the kids? Will it make their bedtime too late?"

"Please, Mama," Matt said. "I don't have to get up early."

"I guess it will be all right. You'll surely be home by nine."

"That's for sure," Dirk said. Then he glanced at Neal. He didn't ask if he wanted to go.

He's letting Neal decide, Mary Anne thought. *But will Papa be hurt if he doesn't go?*

"I think I'd better help," Neal said. "Those crazy Angus! You never can tell which way they'll go."

Mary Anne went upstairs. None of her homework had been squeezed into the full hours of Saturday. She'd outlined two pages of history when the telephone rang. She heard her mother say, "Yes. She's here. I'll call her."

Mary Anne raised her eyebrows as she walked into the kitchen. Her mother answered the unspoken question with a whisper, "I don't know who it is. No one that's called here before."

Roger? Mary Anne thought as she hesitated. For a

second or two she didn't know who responded to her weak "hello." Not until he said, "It's Clay. Or would you have recongized my voice?"

"I don't know," Mary Anne said. "I've never talked to you on the phone."

"Well, this could have waited until morning. But I thought you might like to know." He went on to say that his family had eaten in the university cafeteria at noon and that the Oak Hill principal came in and sat near them.

"We got to talking, so we shoved our tables together," Clay said. "Mainly, he told about this council of kids from the different schools. You know about that."

"Yes, Mr. Davidson talked to me at school."

"Then you know that the plan was to begin operating when the new wing is done. When Springvale kids move in. But that won't be until Thanksgiving. Now they're talking of some meetings before then — the first Tuesday after school."

"That sounds like a good idea to me," Mary Anne said. "By the last of November the people from the other schools could be a little better adjusted. But those from Springvale wouldn't."

The conversation lasted for nearly five minutes. Clay said he was looking forward to the discussion and that he knew a few new students but not well. "Do you know many from Springvale?" he asked.

"Yes. But I don't know how many. People move, you know. But Connie Collins, the one I know best, is still out there."

"Did you go to school with her?"

"Only one year," Mary Anne said. "After she and her father came to live with her aunt — who's really her father's aunt. But they live near my Grandpa Garland, so I see her more."

After she put the receiver on the hook, Mary Anne sat down at the kitchen table and talked to her mother who had the *Sunday Star* spread out over the round surface. She explained the reason for Clay's call, then she rested her chin on a doubled fist and stared out the window, into darkness. "I was just thinking, Connie and I haven't visited each other for a long time. I wonder why."

"Did you have a spat?"

"No," Mary Anne said. "I don't think so. I wrote and asked her to come for my birthday in July but she had to go visit her mother."

"Had to?"

"Well, it was time. But I don't think she really likes to go. She feels her mother didn't want her at the time of the divorce. And that she doesn't now."

"Does she?"

"Connie's not sure. But she knows her mother's new husband doesn't want her around. Never has."

"Poor girl," Susan said.

"I think she's happy now most of the time. Her dad's — well, the way Connie puts it, 'I'm at the hub of his wheel, not flung to the outside rim.'"

"Was that the last time you contacted Connie before your birthday?"

"No. She called me — no, she stopped here once. Right after school started, the day I went to Evansville with Nancy and Grandpa."

"I guess you've just missed one another."

"Is it all right if I call her right now? May I ask her to stay all night with me Friday or Saturday? She could ride in with Papa, if no one's coming this way."

"Go ahead," Susan said. "You do the inviting and Rhoda and I will work out the transportation. I am going out there — say, let *me* talk before you hang up."

Mary Anne placed the call with the operator and as she waited, she said, "Connie could be gone. On a date."

"Does she go with someone?"

"Not steady. And not often, as far as I know. She's like — Oh, hello stranger. I began to think no one was there." Mary Anne explained why she'd called. "Good! Mama's going to Springvale one day. Now she wants to talk to Mrs. Collins. I can't run up the telephone bill. Not right here in the kitchen, with Mama staring at me."

Mary Anne didn't go back upstairs. She decided she could finish her homework after supper, if it wasn't too late. She went to the living room and curled up on the end of the couch. She was a little sleepy, perhaps from walking in the cool air.

She heard the refrigerator door bump shut and the clank of silverware. Then the telephone rang again. *Are we getting suddenly popular?* she thought. She couldn't hear what her mother said. She didn't talk long. *She's coming this way.*

Mary Anne twisted her head sideways and looked at her mother who was smiling as she stood in the archway. "Was it for me?"

"No. It was Mr. Purcell, the insurance man. He wanted to talk to your father. But he thought he was talking to you. Or at least I hope so."

"What do you mean?"

"Well, he said. 'Honey, is your papa there?' "

"That's because we sound alike," Mary Anne said. "Mama, do you think we are that much alike? I mean can you remember how it felt to be sixteen or almost seventeen?"

"Mary Anne Garland! What a question! How could I forget! You are always asking me to tell stories about when I was growing up — the olden times as you call them."

"I don't mean what you did and your clothes and what Grandfather taught you. I mean — what hurt and worried and even scared you."

Susan walked a few steps to the left and sat down in the new brown velvet chair. She was on the fringe of the circle of light and her face was shadowed.

"Are you hurt — or worried — or scared?"

"Sometimes."

"I suppose that's normal. Growing up isn't all learning and developing. Becoming aware of problems and pain and sorrow is a part of the experience of maturing."

Mary Anne heard her mother draw a deep breath. "I've wished so often that I could keep you and Ellen and your brothers in sort of a greenhouse. With walls of glass to let in warmth and light and keep out cold and the darkness of danger. But it wouldn't work."

"Why, Mama? It sounds good to me."

"You'd not survive when you had to go outside. When tomatoes and snapdragons are left in the hothouse too long they wilt and droop when they're transplanted."

Neither spoke for a few minutes. The radiator clanked a couple of times and steam hissed from the valve at one end. "Is this about Patty?" Susan asked.

"No. Not really. I'm getting along fine without her. It's just — there's only one way to say it, I guess. I don't want to go out with boys."

"Is anyone bothering you? Or pushing?"

"No. Not now. But I know what they all think."

"All?" Susan said. "You might be surprised if you could know how many girls — and boys too — feel as you do."

"No one says anything."

"That's the way it is. Each one thinks they're the only one."

"Then how can we ever find out who's not in a mad rush to grow up? Put a notice on the bulletin board?"

"If I said that was a good idea, would you consider it?"

"No. I'd be too embarrassed."

"Certainly you would," Susan said. "And I'd have felt the same way. There is a way though. Watch people. Forget how left out you feel for a while. See if anyone else is wandering off to themselves or studying all noon hour."

"Like I do."

"Yes. Aren't there others?"

"Yes, a few. But they're mainly new kids. I don't know them."

Susan got up when the arc of car lights swept across the wall. "The cowboys have returned." She walked over and ran her fingers down one of Mary Anne's cheeks. "Don't think I don't understand. But remember, I survived."

But you were hurt, Mary Anne thought. *And you never say how or why. Is it because you think I'd be more scared if I knew? Or because you're still trying to protect me?*

She didn't get up from the couch until Little Matt came in and said, "Grandpa sent a cake. Chocolate, your favorite kind."

"Where'd Grandpa get a cake to give away?"

"Some ladies brought them. A whole bunch. Grandpa said if we didn't take one he might have to have a bake sale."

"I'll be out in a minute. My foot's asleep."

"Feel like it has needles sticking in it?"

"Uh-huh."

"They'll go away. I've had that. Don't worry."

Mary Anne smiled. *Little Matt doesn't worry much. Has an answer for everything. Who's he like? Things get handed down in families. I compare feelings to things like Mama and Grandfather Kirk. Mama says Neal's serious like her mother. Is Matt like Papa? But I don't know how he was when he was five. He never tells stories about growing up.*

12

Mary Anne's father was standing at the kitchen window when she went downstairs the next morning. He turned and said, "The frost is on the pumpkins even if the fodder is not in the shock."

"That's from a poem," Mary Anne said. "I never heard you quote James Whitcomb Riley before."

"Nor any other poet," Dirk Garland said. "But lines and verses run through my head now and then. One just popped out."

"It *is* frosty, isn't it?" Mary Anne said. She'd walked to the west window and pulled back a panel of the crossbar dimity curtains. The sunlight was silvered as it filtered through the powder-blue sky. It shone on a world which was iced in whiskery white. The branches and twigs of the redbud tree were upholstered in frosty bristles and the wire clothesline was a necklace of snowy needles.

"It's lovely," Mary Anne said as she turned and smiled at her father. "But I don't see a single pumpkin."

"Neither did I. Not out there. Only in what your Grandfather Kirk calls the mind's eye."

"I guess we see a lot of mental pictures, don't

we?" Mary Anne said. "But not all of them as beautiful as the way the world looks right now."

"Is there something special out there?" Susan asked from the doorway to the cellar. She put the basket of glass jars on the end of the cabinet and walked to the back window.

"See for yourself, Susan," Dirk said. He stepped back and put one hand on her shoulder. "Jack Frost wielded a mighty heavy paintbrush last night."

"I see," Susan said. "Papa would say that Mother Nature is compensating."

"Compensating?"

"Yes. By making the cold world look so lovely we are able to bear the dark days and frigid temperatures."

"Well, I guess there's something to that," Dirk said. "But along about January it gets to seeming that the bad days outnumber the good."

"Papa," Mary Anne said. "Why are you still here? Didn't you say you were going to sell something this morning?"

"I did and we are. Joe Manley, who owns the stock truck, is coming to pick me up in about a quarter of an hour."

"How will you get home?" Susan asked.

"I'm not sure. Pa wants to buy himself a small car. You know he let Ma's big one sell as part of the estate. So we might ride in to Muncie with Joe and look around. Could you come get us if we don't make a deal?"

"Certainly," Susan said. "But don't call me here. Nancy and I are making last-of-the-garden pickles.

I'll be there until after two at least. My goodness! Look at the time! We're going to have to step lively or there'll be a rash of tardiness in the Garland family."

"The boys are up," Mary Anne said. "I heard Matt calling Neal when I came down the hall."

"Then we'd better point Matt in Ellen's direction," Susan said.

Dirk left a few minutes before the others came down for breakfast. As Mary Anne ladled oatmeal into bowls from the bubbling kettle she asked, "Does Grandpa have money? Enough to buy a car? I always thought — "

"That your Grandmother Garland kept a grip on the purse."

"Something like that."

"Well, she did. And no one knew what kind of an arrangement she'd insisted on until after she died — until the will was read. No one but your father."

"Can you tell me?"

"No reason not to," Susan said. "Father Garland was paid like a hired hand, only not as much. Your grandma made it plain that Dirksen money would be managed by Dirksens."

"Is there a lot?"

"Yes. And all of it was left to your father except a quarter of the yearly income for your grandpa. And he was to live there."

"That seems cruel."

"It was. I was heartsick when I heard how she'd left things. Bertha managed her son when she was here. But that will changed his thinking drastically —

sort of turned him around in his tracks. That and other influences. When the estate was settled, half of everything was put in Grandpa Garland's name — by your father. Which is no more than was fair."

"When did you find out about all of this, Mama? We didn't live out there then."

"I know," Susan said. "It was your father who told me. Just before he came to Oak Hill to live with us."

"There's a lot you're not saying, isn't there?" Mary Anne asked.

"Yes. You've been aware of that lately, haven't you?"

"Well, questions sort of flit in and out of my mind. Some stay a while."

"I guess that's natural. And in time I'll be able to answer some of them anyway. Now we must get *this* day on the way."

Mary Anne thought more about money on the way to school than she had in a long time. Did they have a lot? She knew her mother had a checkbook of her own and that they had a good car and a new truck. *But Neal still runs his paper route and Mama makes a lot of the clothes Ellen and I wear. Grandmother Garland's money doesn't seem to have made much change in the way we live.*

She saw Carmelita ahead of her as she came within sight of the building. At first Mary Anne didn't recognize her because her long black hair was piled up on top of her head, not curling around her shoulders as usual. "Hey, 'Lita! Wait — I didn't know you! Your hair looks — I can't find the word. But I like it. You're beautiful."

"I am?" Carmelita said. "No one's ever said that to me before. But I can tell you how I *hope* this hair-do looks."

"How?"

"Stunning. They're having tryouts for the Drama and Song Club production. The first play calls for a stunning brunette with a Spanish accent. The accent I have. The stunning I have to fake."

"Well, I don't know as that's true. You look great — for real. But I didn't know you were interested in acting."

"Good reason," Carmelita said. "I've never done any except for my sisters and in the migrant camp, I put on a lot of shows down there for the little kids while their mothers were in the tomato fields."

"I hope you get the part," Mary Anne said. "Want me to pray for you?"

"Oh, would you? Do you know something? This is the first time anyone in Oak Hill — besides people like me — has mentioned prayer to me. Maybe it's because we go to different churches."

"Maybe," Mary Anne said. "But God's the same, isn't He?"

I sure hope she gets the part, Mary Anne thought as she went on to class. *I have the feeling she'll be a good actress and doing well might make her feel more — more included.*

The activities of the next two days kept Mary Anne busy. Roger's ridicule and her fading friendship with Patty were on the outer edge of her experience. By the end of the first discussion session of representatives of the four schools in the consolidation, she felt more in place than she had for months.

"Actually," she told her mother late that afternoon, "I knew this was a good idea from the beginning. But as soon as I walked into the room the whole project became personally wonderful. Guess who represents Springvale. Guess one."

"Let me think — could it be Connie?"

"Yes. Isn't that great?"

"She didn't mention this last night, did she?"

"No. But neither did I."

"Who's the other one? Anyone we know?"

"Well, yes," Mary Anne said. "But I didn't recognize him at first. It's amazing how someone can change in 4 1/2 years."

"I've noticed," Susan said. "But who do you mean?"

"Steven Corwin. Remember him?"

"Certainly. His family lives south of Springvale, beyond the Garland land."

"The kids used to call him bean pole, which was cruel. I never did, even though he was tall and thin, even skinny. But not now. He's so good-looking. And he remembered me. Connie says he goes steady with someone, which is a relief."

"It is?"

"Yes, it is. When are we going to eat? I'm starved."

"Then you'd better grab a snack. I'm about ready to go to Muncie. Your grandpa hasn't made up his mind about a car. Wants to sleep on the matter. So I'm going in — running the taxi. Want to go?"

"No, I have homework. And who'd look after Matt?"

"Oh, he's going. Been out in the car for at least twenty minutes. He's blown the horn four times."

Mary Anne made three graham cracker and peanut butter sandwiches to take to her room. She munched on them as she wrote an answer to Lois' invitation. "Mama says I can come with the Masters," she wrote. "What will we be doing? What kind of clothes should I bring?"

As she sealed the letter she realized her feelings about the trip had changed a little. *I still want to go. I like Lois already. And I think we'll have fun. But I'm not quite so miserable here. What Patty and Roger say, think, and do doesn't matter. Not much anyway.*

She'd read nearly half of the assignment for contemporary literature class when the doorbell rang. She was a third of the way downstairs before she realized she was barefooted. By the time she went back for her shoes and got to the hall, whoever had been there was gone. She opened the door and looked both ways. No one was in sight except Cissy Crandall who lived across the street. She was on the next to the top step of a ladder cleaning leaves out of a rainspout. "It couldn't have been her."

"Probably a salesman or someone asking where somebody lives. If it had been important they'd have waited."

But she couldn't help wondering who'd rung the bell. *I feel the same way every time I hear the ring of the telephone. Who is it? Who do they want? It's sort of exciting, an expectancy, I guess.*

When Neal came home she learned who'd pushed the ivory button at the side of the front door.

"Where you been? Or did you just get home?"

"I've been here an hour. Why?"

"Well, I saw Roger Trent. He was going in the drugstore. He asked where you were."

Mary Anne's face felt warm as she said, "I'm nowhere as far as he's concerned. Nowhere!"

13

Mary Anne saw Roger three or four times during the next week but he didn't approach her or even speak. She came to the conclusion that he hadn't stopped to see her after she heard the seniors were selling subscriptions to magazines. The information came from Clay Gilbert at noon on Wednesday.

"Seems like this is getting to be a custom," Clay said as he pulled out a chair across the table from Mary Anne.

"What is? Eating?"

"That too," Clay said. "But I meant the fact that this chair is empty."

"Do chairs have customs?"

Clay grinned as he set baked chili, rolls, and tossed salad on the table.

"Sometimes you sound like Mr. Kirk. When you are in a teasing or even a serious mood."

"I didn't know you knew my grandfather that well. You couldn't have been in any of his classes."

"I wasn't. He retired before I got to high school. But I got a double promotion back in the grades. And it wasn't such a good idea. I needed help. So Mr. Kirk gave me a boost now and then."

"I've been wondering why you were taking driver's training this year," Mary Anne said.

"Because I'm just now old enough. But that's not what I want to talk about. Has anyone seen your mother about subscribing to magazines?"

"No. Not that I know about."

Clay went on to say that the town had been blocked off. "Roger had your square and I — well I figured he might not want to face your folks, thinking they'd know he's been sort of persecuting you."

Mary Anne didn't look up. She set her plate to one side and reached for the small bowl of quivering Jello cubes. But her mind was doing what Neal called "clicking in high gear." *So Roger did stop at our house but he probably saw Mama leave and thought no one was at home. So he rang the bell and left. That way he can report he tried. He didn't want to see me at all. That's a relief.*

For some reason (or perhaps more than one) Mary Anne didn't tell Clay that Roger had stopped. "Mama will probably take some. What are you raising money for? The class trip?"

"Yes," Clay said. "But there's some doubt if we'll go."

"I thought seniors always went to New York."

"Well, they have. But some parents like mine aren't sure the money's well spent. No, that's not quite right. It's the time and opportunity they feel is wasted."

"I know what you mean. Grandfather was a sponsor once. No one ever coaxed him to go again. He said it was like trying to drive a crooked nail to get kids to go to museums or attend concerts. They either wanted to go skating or see a movie that'd be in Muncie when they got home."

"Yes. I've heard all the arguments."

"How do you feel?"

"Mixed up," Clay said. "I see both sides but this is the thing that makes me drag my feet about all these money-raising projects. To tell you the truth, I'm sort of a misfit in my class."

"Because you're younger?"

"Maybe. But sometimes I feel a lot older. I hope you know what I mean. I won't try to explain."

"I know," Mary Anne said. She thought of the day she'd watched the men building fence. "The boundary line between being a teenager and an adult is sort of wavy, I guess."

"You said it! And now I've got to move along. It's time for — "

"I know, driver's training."

As Mary Anne left the cafeteria she couldn't help wondering if Clay was gradually working toward the point of asking her to go out with him. She hoped not. *I like him and feel comfortable with him now. But dating might change things.*

She remembered what Connie Collins had said about her first date. "It was a miserable awkward experience. I'd known this boy for years. Went to school with him until we moved to Springvale. Then I saw him every summer when I went back for my *house-divided* days."

Mary Anne had interrupted by asking, "Your what?"

"Oh, you know what Lincoln said, 'A house divided cannot stand.' Anyway, as I was saying, the minute

Darrel and I were alone I felt like a fish out of water, a square peg in a round hole — anything but in the right place. And do you know something? I think he felt the same way."

"I wonder why," Mary Anne said.

"I guess we felt like we had to play a role, act a part, and we didn't know the lines," Connie said. "I wonder if anyone's ever taken a survey on this. To find out how many people can stand each other after that first date. Darrel and I couldn't."

Mary Anne smiled as she opened a locker door. *If Connie's theory is correct it would be a good idea for everyone to pick out someone they don't like very well for their first date. Not ruin a good friendship. But why am I thinking like this? I don't want to go with anyone. Not yet, anyway.*

A cold rain was coming slantwise from the east when Connie came to Oak Hill with Mary Anne's father. He was earlier than usual that evening. The soil in the cornfield was sticky soon after the rain began. "The tractor and picker tires were miring down and the wet stalks kept choking up the machinery," Dirk said at the table.

"I hope you and Father Garland don't get reckless," Susan said. "Almost every week in the fall I read where someone's lost a hand or an arm or even their life."

"That's because they're in too big a hurry. It doesn't take more than an extra minute or two to shut off the motor and restart it."

"Did you go into the little barn?" Neal asked. "Has Grandpa changed anything since Saturday?"

"Well, let's see," his father said. "The answer to your first question is yes. I go in not once — to eat lunch — but two or more times every day. Pa thinks of something he wants me to help move from the big house."

"Like what, Papa?" Mary Anne asked.

"First it was the china cupboard. The one with curved glass on all three sides."

"Father Garland wanted that?" Susan said. "That surprises me."

"I felt the same way," Dirk said. "But he told me he got the idea on Sunday night. The folks, neighbors, and friends had gone home. He'd built a big fire and was sitting staring at the flames. Someone had left a dish of fruit on the table, a cut-glass dish. Pa noticed how the firelight made it sparkle. So right then and there he got the notion of moving the china cupboard and putting it on the north wall. And that's where it is."

"Did you move the dishes?" Mary Anne asked.

"Nope," her father said. "That's a job for someone not so clumsy. I held my breath for fear we'd smash one of the glasses in that cupboard. I don't know as they could be replaced. Pa said he'd content himself with watching the reflections of the fire in the glass of the doors until you could get out there, Susan."

"That'll be Sunday," Susan answered. "You tell him we'll come as soon as we can get there after church." Then she turned to Connie. "You can go with us, can't you?"

"I think so," Connie said. "Unless Daddy decides to

go up to Lake Chapman to close our cottage for the winter."

"You got two homes?" Little Matt asked.

"In a way," was all Connie said. Mary Anne knew what her friend was thinking. She'd once confided her torn feelings in these words, "Sometimes I don't know if I have three homes or none."

"I only got one home," Matt said. "Right here."

"Isn't that enough for you?" Dirk asked.

"Yes," the little boy said. "It's just fine."

Mary Anne glanced at her mother. She was smiling. Her eyes were a little misty but there was no sadness in them. Not this time.

"Any of you want to go gadding?" Dirk Garland asked.

"I do," Ellen said. "Where?"

"How do you know if you want to go before you know where?" Neal asked.

"I just like to go places," Ellen said. "Papa never has taken me any place I didn't want to be."

Mary Anne saw her father shake his head, as if he was in pain, flinching. "I wish everyone I know could say the same," he said without looking at anyone except Susan.

"Anyone want a second piece of pie?" Susan said quickly. "How about you, Dirk? You've been out in the cold."

"Thank you. I'll take another one, Susan," Mary Anne's father said. "I don't know but what butterscotch is my favorite pie."

"Oh, Papa," Ellen said. "Last week you said you liked cherry best."

105

"That was last week," Dirk said. "And this is now. Say! Somebody tell me. How did we get to the subject of cherry pie? I asked if anyone wanted to go — "

"And I do," Susan said. "I've been hearing about the new shopping center over at Anderson. I don't have anything I particularly need. But it might be fun to go."

"I heard about that. It's all enclosed. You kids could roam around without much chance of getting lost. You might be misplaced for a while but not lost permanently."

By the time the Garlands reached the city in Madison County it was only an hour and a half until closing time. Connie and Mary Anne raced to visit every shop that surrounded the center mall. They didn't do much more than step inside a few stores but they stayed several minutes in the dress shops and longer than that in the bookstore. "Do you suppose books are coming back in style?" Connie asked. "There's not a store like this at home now. Only way out at the college."

"Could be," Mary Anne said.

Little Matt pouted on the way home because he didn't get to stay in the pet store as long as he wanted. "We *were* there nearly an hour," Neal said, "He looked at every single goldfish, and two puppies took naps and woke up before I drug him down to the hobby shop."

"What did you get, Mama?" Mary Anne asked. "You were carrying sacks."

"She was carrying sacks," Dirk said. "Didn't you see how burdened your poor father was."

"I know what you had," Mary Anne said. "Blankets. It said so on the end of the boxes."

"I got a couple of remnants," Susan said. "They'll make nice skirts for Ellen."

"What are you going to do when all of us get too big for what a remnant will make?" Mary Anne asked. "What fun will it be for you to find a bargain?"

"I'll find a reason probably," Susan said. "Once the remnant fever gets into a person's blood, there's no cure. But I picked up a few other things, including a copper teakettle. For your Grandpa Garland."

"But, Mom. He has one," Neal said. "I moved it, and sloshed water all over me."

"But it's graniteware and chipped in several places," Susan said. "And this one will look nice, sitting on the hearth."

"Seems to me this family is getting another kind of fever," Dirk said. "For fireplaces. All of you sort of light up when Pa's fireplace is mentioned. Maybe we ought to have one."

"Could we?" Susan asked. "I've been thinking about the idea. And trying to picture one on each wall in every room."

"Mama," Ellen said. "That would be thirty-two fireplaces!"

"I didn't mean that," Susan said. "I was just trying to decide where *one* should be placed. If we had one."

"Not *if*, Susan," Dirk said. "*When*. You keep on thinking and we'll get the man over, the one who built Pa's. Let his know-how help you decide."

As they turned off the state road and headed toward Oak Hill, Neal said, "Ellen, I've been trying to figure out something. If you can multiply 4 x 8 and come out with the right answer, why am I always helping you with your arithmetic?"

"Because," Ellen said. "It's easier to ask you. It makes me tired to do a whole bunch of thinking."

14

Whenever Mary Anne had time to think of how she'd let Patty and what Roger said upset her, she felt a little ashamed. *That's like a fourth-grader would react. Pouting because someone wouldn't play with me or crying around because someone called me names. What if Roger did mean something bad when he called me Mama's girl? People say a lot of bad things about others — all the time.*

Such thoughts came to her now and then but didn't linger. She had better things to do with her mind. The group of representatives from the four schools, now called the Friendly Forum, became the nucleus for a larger group which planned an all-school mixer for the Thanksgiving vacation. Springvale students were to move in the next Monday.

As Connie Collins said at the second meeting, "If everyone knew even one or two people from the other schools, maybe we wouldn't pull off from the others in little cliques."

"But don't we?" Clay asked. "I mean I already knew a few kids from other places. People I met in 4-H and at church camp."

"Well, so did I," Mary Anne said. "But I still had

the tendency just to speak to them and go on. I suppose they seemed like — "

"Outsiders?" Connie asked.

"I guess that's right," Mary Anne said. "I was about to say visitors. That sounds a little kinder."

During the planning meetings the eight people who were working for a common purpose seemed to be welded together or as Clay put it, integrated. *I suppose when you come right down to it there is more than one kind of segregation.*

Mary Anne looked forward to the time when she'd be able to eat in the cafeteria with Connie and meet her between classes. But she already felt warm toward the other three girls in the group, especially Martie Connor who lived in Mt. Summit. They were in two classes together but hadn't spoken until the Friendly Forum was formed.

Martie was tall and had hair almost the color of a new penny. She'd had it cut soon after school started. It curled around her head like a copper halo. "I'm not in style here," she told Mary Anne. "Everyone here has ponytails or long pageboys."

"Not everyone," Mary Anne said.

"You're right," Martie said. "My mother says I use that word with reckless abandon. Meaning, when I want to do something I use the argument that every one is. Which they aren't. If you know what I mean."

"I know. When I say that, my mama pins me down and has me name who everyone includes."

"I know your mother," Martie said. "Well, in a way I do. She and my aunt were friends — still are, I guess."

110

"Who's your aunt?"

"She was Lillian Connor. My father's sister. They lived in Oak Hill until my father was out of college. He knew your mother too. My mom still teases him about her, saying Susan Kirk was his first love."

"Was she?" Mary Anne asked. "I've heard Mama mention your aunt often, and your father sometimes, but she never said they went together."

"I'm not sure they did — not much anyway. But my mother got the idea somehow that Dad liked your mother a lot. He says you look just like her."

"Where did he see me?"

"At the end of the walk. He picks me up after Friendly Forum, on the way home from Muncie. He teaches there."

Mary Anne thought about the conversation several times that evening. She didn't mention it to her mother because there wasn't time. Susan was ready to leave for her class and barely took time to say that the hamburgers were ready to be fried and escalloped potatoes were in the oven. "I didn't get a dessert made," she said. "I worked all afternoon on those two critical reports. There's money on the table. You can buy something."

As she walked upstairs Mary Anne thought, *Mama always seems a little different on class night. Like someone I don't know quite as well. Sort of like she's playing a different part. Is this more like the way she was before she was married? Back when Martie's father thought she was something special?*

She put her corduroy jumper on a hanger and took the round-collared blouse downstairs with her. It needed to be sponged in mild suds. The house was still. Neal was on his paper route and Little Matt was helping Grandpa Kirk haul scraps of wood home from the lumberyard.

Mary Anne walked through the study and living room. The feel of home was all around her. *My room is the same as when we left the farm. Mama's made a lot of changes down here, but nothing seems strange. Probably because she bought one thing at a time and did a lot of thinking between purchases.* She'd heard her mother say, "It takes a while for a chair or a couch or a table to blend with a room — or into our picture of home."

She recalled the evening she'd heard about her mother's favorite ways of playing. *I must have been about ten and was complaining that I didn't have anything to do. Mama and I were sitting on the back step, the one which wasn't broken, and Neal was pumping water for the calves — when there was no breeze to turn the blades of the windmill we had to pump by hand.*

She remembered that her mother asked, "Isn't it time for you to relieve your brother?"

"This is his last turn. The tank's finally full."

The world seemed lonely that night, Mary Anne thought. *And I don't know why. It was one of those times when I peeked ahead into growing up and it didn't seem like much fun.*

"What can I do?" Mary Anne had asked. "It's a long time before I have to go to bed."

"Tired of your paper dolls already?"

"No. Not exactly. I played with them about two

hours. If I keep on I will be tired. Then what could I do?"

"You could try shopping out of the catalog. Grandpa brought us one last week." She told how when she was a little girl she pretended she had a certain amount of money and spent it on things from the catalog in her imagination. "I wrote all the prices down and figured and figured so the money and my order would come out even."

Mary Anne liked that idea. She'd mentally furnished many rooms after that evening. *That's what I seemed to enjoy most. Maybe I'll be an interior decorator.*

As she put food on the table, she heard raindrops splattering on the kitchen window. By the time the dishes were washed, the shower had increased to a downpour. "Driving won't be easy for your mother," Dirk said as he walked to the front door and turned on the porch light. "Tarvia roads are black when they're wet and chilly as it is, the windows will like as not fog up."

"Mama's careful," Neal said.

"I know but she'll not be the only one on the road."

"You don't have to worry, Papa," Matt said. "Every time we start out Mama prays for God to make her careful for *two* people."

"How do you know this?" Mary Anne asked.

"'Cause I hear her. She whispers, 'Please make us careful — me and the person I meet.' But I can hear. Her whispered prayers are pretty loud."

"Well, I guess we don't have to worry, do we?" Neal said. And Mary Anne, feeling a rush of tenderness for her little brother, asked if he'd like her to read a story. He was asleep before Susan came home and those who had been uneasy went to bed, all except Mary Anne.

"Hadn't you better scoot upstairs?" Susan asked.

"In a minute," Mary Anne said. She walked to the foot of the stairway to see if her father had gone all the way to the second floor. For some reason she didn't think her mother would answer the question which was in her mind if he was near.

She led up to it by saying, "I had a long talk with a girl in the Friendly Forum today."

"Your discussion group, is that what it's called, officially?"

"Oh, no. That's our name."

"But I interrupted. What were you going to say?"

"She knows you — I mean her aunt and father do. She's Martie Connor."

"Not Ray's daughter. Do they live near here?"

"Over at Mt. Summit."

"The last I heard they were up in Tippecanoe County near Lafayette."

"Did — I mean Martie seems to think her father liked you a lot."

As Mary Anne waited for her mother to speak, she kept her eyes on her face. *Is she blushing or is her face rosy from the color of the lampshade?*

"Did he?" Mary Anne prompted.

"Well, I don't really know. But I used to wish he did. He was so handsome but terribly shy. That's an unusual combination. Girls often make boys like Ray conceited."

"By running after them?"

"Yes. That still goes on?"

"It does," Mary Anne said. "But go on. About Martie's father."

"There's nothing more to say. He went off to college — to DePauw and I rarely saw him. Not at all after I went to Springvale to live."

Mary Anne bit her lips on other questions. Did you like him? Do you think about him? Is this part of the trouble between you and Papa? She sensed that there was no use to ask. *I just know Mama wouldn't answer.*

"Did Ray's daughter say what he does now?" Susan asked. "He worked as a chemist when he graduated. Lillian hasn't written to tell me he'd changed jobs or that they lived nearby."

"He's teaching. In Muncie, I think."

"That's good," Susan said. "That's what he aimed to do. Then the big money job sidetracked him. And, *you've* sidetracked me! It's half an hour past your bedtime."

Mary Anne was tired but she didn't go to sleep for a while. Questions and possibilities chased each other in her mind. *What would have happened if Mr. Connor hadn't been so shy? He might have married Mama and she'd be a teacher's wife. Did she get tired of waiting for him to pay attention to her? She might have gone out with Papa to make this Ray Connor jealous. And if Mama had married him, would I be me? That's a silly question. I wouldn't even be!*

15

Mary Anne felt in place wherever she went now, even at school. She spoke to boys she knew, stopped and talked to a few without thinking that they might get the idea that she was wanting them to ask her to go out with them. No one did, not even Clay Gilbert, although she ate with him a few times, and they sometimes walked home from school as far as the intersection of Maple and Walnut streets. But this seemed natural. There wasn't time during the school day to do all the planning for the four-school mixer. And the Friendly Forum meetings sometimes went on until after dark now that late fall had come to central Indiana.

The first snow fell in early November. Mary Anne was sitting in fifth period study hall when she first noticed flakes sifting through the air. By the time school was dismissed the ground and streets were covered and the snowfall was a thick curtain which kept descending until long after dark.

Little Matt was transported into a world of pure joy. He didn't want to take time to eat and fought against going to bed. He played outside until every pair of mittens and canvas gloves that came close to fitting him were wet. His mother said he had to wait until the radiator had time to sizzle the melted snow out of those he'd worn first.

Even after dark, Matt kept checking on the weather. He ran to the front door, turned on the porch light, and waited until a car crept along Maple Street. "It's still snowing," he said. "I can see it in front of the lights."

Neal was on the floor working on a relief map of the farm. He'd kneaded green clay and pressed it onto a plywood square, within the outlines of the pasture field and the barn lot. He was working a brown ball to be spread over the rectangle which marked the plowed corn ground. Every time Matt dashed through the room, Neal leaned protectively over his project. "That kid!" he said after the fourth trip to the lookout post. "He acts as if he thinks snow has gone out of style. If he steps on this green clay I'll have mountains where prairies are suppose to be."

"You could move your board over here," Mary Anne said. "Away from Matt's racetrack."

"Yes. But the light shines on my glasses over there, instead of on what I'm doing."

"Snow makes me restless too," Mary Anne's father said. "But not for the same reason. Matt's afraid it will stop. I'm wishing it would. Or wondering if the wind will rise in the night."

"And cause drifting," Susan said. "I was thinking about that. Do you know if your father had groceries on hand?"

"He does but he didn't," Dirk said. "He told me he was spreading clean straw in the calf stalls when warning of the approaching snowfall came from the barn radio. "So I poked around in Pa's kitchen. Then I jumped in the truck, went by Rhoda's, and we drove into Springvale."

"You and Grandpa?" Ellen asked.

"No. Rhoda and I. Your Grandpa was making Christmas presents in the shop."

"What? Who for?" Matt asked.

"That stopped you in your race to the front door, didn't it?" Dirk said. "Well, you might as well go on. I can't tell you what or who for."

"What made you think of going by Rhoda's?" Susan asked. "Had you heard that she was sick or something?"

"No. But Joe's down in Lexington at some kind of conference for insurance agents. And I didn't figure Mrs. Collins would want to get out on the roads after the snow began to pepper down."

"Snow wouldn't pepper, Papa," Ellen said. "It's white. It would salt."

"I thought you never talked like a dictionary," Neal said.

"I'm glad you thought of Rhoda, Dirk," Susan said, ignoring Neal's remark. "That was nice."

"Don't give credit where it's not due. In the first place, I figure I owe her. And in the second, that lady is like a tonic in spring. Perks you up."

Susan nodded her head in agreement.

"I think this would be a good night to make popcorn balls," Mary Anne said.

"Any night is good for that," Ellen agreed.

"Not according to Rhoda," Mary Anne replied.

"Don't you remember the night she stayed all night with us? Papa, I think you were snowed in at Grandma's. Rhoda brought us bread and stuff and nearly got stuck in a drift."

"I remember," Susan said. "We raised strawberry popcorn that year. It took eight or nine of those little ears to make a bowl of balls."

"And Rhoda said it was a good time to make them because we could set the bowl in the snow and cool the hot syrup in a hurry."

It was nearly bedtime by the time the snow on the back step cooled the balls the Garlands ate that night. The gusts of wind kept increasing in force. They shrieked past the windows. Mary Anne pulled back the marquisette curtains at the east window. The glass was plastered with snow.

She thought of the lines she'd memorized the year before from Whittier's poem, "Snowbound." She remembered phrases like, "The wind blew east: we heard the roar," and "the white drift piled the window frame."

"This is one time I wish I'd gone deliberately against Pa's wishes and had a telephone put in for him," Dirk said.

"Why doesn't Grandpa want one?" Ellen asked.

"He says it would disturb his peace. Make him jumpy. That looking at a phone on the wall would be kind of a threat. He'd never know when it might ring or what kind of bad news it would bring."

"I've been thinking about something," Susan said. She put down the red and blue plaid skirt she'd been hemming and tucked a strand of hair into the coronet of brown braids. "Knowing Father Garland's out there alone on a night like this makes me wonder if we should move onto the farm — to be near him."

Mary Anne was startled. *Or am I shocked?* The idea of leaving Oak Hill had occurred to her but mother had never even hinted that this might happen. *This is home,* she thought. *I was sure Mama felt the same way — that this was the reason she brought us here.*

She looked at Neal and he dropped his eyes. She knew he shared her feelings. *He never liked working on the farm. Why I wonder? He enjoys going out there now.*

Dirk was the first to speak on the idea of moving. "Is this something you'd like, Susan?"

"No. I have to say no — for myself. But don't we owe your father something? In the way of companionship and affection?"

Dirk had taken off his laced work shoes and put on a pair of ribbed wool socks. Mary Anne could hear the whisper they made as her father moved one foot back and forth in the beige and brown rug.

"Don't you think Pa has that now?" Dirk asked. "Not only from us. He's got neighbors. More people stop by in a week to pass the time of day with him than in six months or more when I was growing up. No, Susan, whatever we might think we owe him, Pa'd say we've paid in full and with high interest besides. The decision about where we live is up to you "

"Should it be, Dirk?" Susan asked. "It has to be harder on you to make these trips back to Eminence Township every day."

"Do you hear me kicking? I get here every night, don't I?"

Mary Anne felt as if her sense of hearing was turned up high, like the knob on a radio. *They're really talking, about problems. Not just about the weather, or getting a new roof, or planting a garden. I never in my whole life heard them do this before. Maybe they have, but not in front of us.*

"Yes, you do," Susan said.

"And what's more," Dirk went on, "I'm a lot more regular than when I lived a mile and a half away."

"But that's not saying you wouldn't rather live out there," Susan said. "Only that it's not a hardship to travel back and forth."

Dirk scratched his temple with one forefinger. "Up till now it's been either you or me who decide where we live. Now there are others who have a right to say how they feel." He looked at Neal. "Speak your mind. This is not a time for saying what you think someone else expects of you."

"Okay," Neal said. "I like it here."

"Mary Anne?" Dirk asked.

"Well, Papa, maybe I could adjust. But this is home. If all the rest of you wanted to move, though, I'd go along."

"Papa," Ellen said, "whatever you and Mama decide is all right with me."

"Should we ask Matt?" Dirk asked.

Susan shook her head. The little boy had climbed up on the couch and his eyes were shut. "He's too sleepy to know what he wants. And too young, perhaps."

"No. I'm not," Matt said. He held his eyes open long enough to say, "I like the way we are now. Besides, there's a Grandpa here. He'd miss us."

"Well, I guess that settles the matter," Dirk said. "No one voted to go."

"But you didn't express your opinion at all," Susan said. "Shouldn't we hear how you feel?"

"Well, I can tell you how I feel. I never want to live in Ma's house again. But I don't know as I'm ready to put the reason into words. Maybe I never will be. Now — I'd better go throw some coal in the furnace. This wind makes a house mighty hard to heat."

Mary Anne's room was chilly in spite of the hissing, clanking radiator. It was on the northeast corner in the path of the wintry gale. Her mother brought a puffy comforter and tucked it under the sides of the mattress. "This smells a little of mothballs," she said. "Your Grandmother Kirk made it of wool scraps, and I have to keep it protected from being meals for moths."

She leaned over and kissed Mary Anne's cheeks. "You're going to bed with an unusually happy feeling, aren't you?"

"Yes. How could you tell?"

"Oh, I saw the shine in your eyes. And another clue — I feel the same way."

"Are you happy, Mama? Truly?"

"Yes, I am."

"But you haven't always been. I can remember lots of times when you seemed sad — or worried."

"I didn't hide my feelings then?"

"Not always. But you know something? Even when you had problems on your mind and were worried, you didn't stop being good to us. You weren't grouchy."

Susan patted Mary Anne's foot through the two blankets and the patchwork comforter.

"Don't give me credit for that. You weren't responsible for my troubles. You were my salvation — my reason for trying to solve them."

After her mother left the room, Mary Anne snuggled down in the cotton and wool nest of her bed. She was more aware than ever that her mother had undergone many trials. *But why am I not quite so scared of what could be ahead of me?*

She drifted off into sleep before another question came to her mind or before an answer came to the first one. For a short time she was aware of the whistling wind and the rattling windows. Then she was covered by a blanket of deep sleep.

16

No classes met at Oak Hill School the next day. Mary Anne was one of the dozen or more people who plunged through the drifts. Because of her habit of being early, she missed hearing the announcement on the radio that all schools in the county, outside of Muncie, were closed.

There were no car tracks on Maple Street. The night winds had whirled snow into drifts, which were higher than her head in places. *It's like I'm the only one in this pure white world,* she thought as she zigzagged trying to find a path where snow wasn't deeper than her boot tops. She glanced across the street and saw the Anthonys' brown and white beagle struggling to cross the yard. *He's in to his nose,* she thought. *If I'd leave him up there, there'd be a puppy angel in the snow. Like when we used to fall backward with arms outspread. The trick was to let two people pull us up so carefully that the angel imprint was not disturbed.*

She decided that the little beagle could never make his way to the house alone. She detoured and carried him to the front steps, where she left him shivering on the woven straw doormat.

An orange delivery truck, from Riggins Dairy in

Muncie, crept across Maple Street on Walnut as Mary Anne approached the intersection. *How'd he get out here?* She thought. Then she realized that the state highway tried to keep Road 3 open.

She began to suspect that school would be closed when she turned the corner. Only two cars were parked beyond the white stakes at the end of the building. One was Mr. Davidson's. He lived straight south of Oak Hill. By this time buses usually began to roar in from all directions. She thought of going back home. *But since I'm this close, I might as well go on. I can get my other textbooks from the locker.*

Her steps made hollow echoes in the empty halls. The only light she saw was at the end of the west wing, where the offices were located. She heard the telephone ring. *People are probably calling to see if there is school today.*

As she reached into her locker she heard two boys talking. The old pattern of dread asserted itself. Could it be Roger? Then reason took over. He'd not be here if there was the slightest chance that there'd be no school. The steps clacked past the lockers and went in the direction of the industrial arts department.

She decided to check at the office to be sure there were no classes before struggling back through the drifts. Four younger girls were coming through the wide doors as she turned toward the office area. "I told you," one said. "The radio announcer said no county schools."

"But this is Oak Hill, not county," another answered.

"County's outside of Muncie, Lela. How many times do I have to explain?"

Mary Anne hesitated. There was no reason to go to the office or to stay in the building. *I feel sort of unanchored,* she thought. *I don't know what to do with myself — except go home. And what's to do there?*

More people were out on the sidewalks and streets by the time she got back to the intersection. One boy was pulling another on a sled, making the first tracks on Maple. Mr. Whalen was shoveling snow from the sidewalk in front of the post office. He stopped with a heaped shovel at arm's length as Mary Anne came along. "I don't know where to dump this," he said. "I guess I'll put it in the street and let the county road department dispose of it."

"The mail truck hasn't come yet, has it?"

"No. And may not for a while. This is one of the times we'd be better off if the old interurban cars still ran. Snow didn't often stop them. Ice on the trolley lines did now and then. Sometimes a person can't tell if progress puts us ahead or behind."

Mary Anne had been expecting a letter from Lois Masters, whose family had been called to Oregon because of the critical illness of Mrs. Masters' mother. The telegram came the evening before Mary Anne was to go to Indianapolis for a visit. She'd had only a postcard from Lois since the visit had to be postponed.

As she came to the general store, Mary Anne decided to call and ask if her mother needed any groceries.

"Don't give me a big order," she said when Susan answered. "I only have a dollar and twenty six — no, twenty-eight cents."

"That's enough. Bring three cakes of yeast and two

pounds of brown sugar. Being snowbound always puts me in the breadmaking mood."

"But we're not snowbound," Mary Anne said. "Not technically. I'm at the store."

"Well, I'm penned in," Susan said. "You know I'm as awkward as a cow with a crutch when it's slippery. Since I'm the breadmaker, this is a good day for baking."

Clay Gilbert came into the store as Mr. Hiatt counted Mary Anne's change into her hand. "You've been to school, haven't you?" Clay asked.

Mary Anne nodded. "How'd you know?"

"I saw you from a distance. I was shoveling our front walk when I caught a glimpse of your red coat."

"Do I have the only red coat in Oak Hill?"

"I don't know of anyone else who goes to school ahead of time. Especially when there is no school."

"I don't know why our radio wasn't — Wait a minute! It was. I heard the market reports as I left the house."

"The announcement came after that. I guess a couple of bus drivers started, then called in when they saw how bad it was. Mr. Davidson told my mother that this was one thing he had to learn to manage as a principal. In big cities, school goes on no matter how few show up."

Mary Anne had her hand on the door when Clay asked, "What are you going to do with yourself today?"

"I don't know. I was wondering myself."

"Well, I walked down Walnut Street a little way to where I could see the hill. Sledding might be good by afternoon. This sun will melt the top and make it slick."

"That sounds like fun," Mary Anne said. "Neal has a sled. It's probably rusty, though."

"Tell him to use some steel wool and come out about one. Call anyone you think might be interested."

Mary Anne's thoughts were a mixture of pleasure and anticipation with a dash of suspicion. Sledding on the hill at the end of Walnut Street had been fun since she'd lived in Oak Hill. No one planned for these outings. No one could. Indiana weather was too unpredictable to announce sledding for a certain day. The idea snowballed when the temperature changed the falling moisture to white flakes. This time Clay was the one who was spreading the word.

On the surface this is probably true. Maybe that's all that's in Clay's mind. But I keep having this feeling that he's going to ask me for a date. That this party is another step in that direction.

But I don't understand, she thought as she braced herself with one hand against the front door frame and took off her boots. *If I think this is going to happen, why am I so eager to go this afternoon?*

The living room seemed dark as she crossed the hall. *I must have a slight case of snow blindness.* Her eyes were adjusted by the time she reached the kitchen. Her mother was standing at the stove.

"Where's everyone?" Mary Anne asked.

"Your father's making a cave in the drift at the back of the lot. Matt and Ellen are probably nagging him to hurry. And Neal's upstairs."

"I'll go up and talk to him. I saw Clay. Oak Hill's having the first sledding party of the winter."

"Well, I don't suppose there'll ever be a better day," Susan said.

Mary Anne left the kitchen, turned and walked back to the door. "Mama," she said. "I keep getting the feeling that Clay's going to ask me for a date."

"That's not unusual. Girls have had such feelings before."

"But that's not all. I don't know whether I'd say yes or no."

"I wouldn't worry too much," Susan said. "The instincts that tell you what Clay's thinking may tell you what to do when you're called on for an answer."

Can a person trust instincts? Mary Anne thought as she climbed the stairs. *What does that word mean anyway?* She stopped in her room before going to talk to Neal. She opened the dictionary before she hung her red coat in the closet. She ran her finger down the column of definitions and read, "An inborn pattern of activity, innate impulse, or natural inclination."

Well, that helps — a little. My impulse is to go with Clay — if he asks me. But what may happen scares me. Like the girls who mess up their lives. And people who get divorces or are unhappy in marriage. Did they let instinct guide them? Or something else?

Neal was putting the finishing touches on the relief map of the farm. He'd dyed crumbles of sponge a deep green and was gluing them to the wooded area and the grove behind the house. "They really look like trees," Mary Anne said. "From here."

"Well I hope they stick," Neal said. "I'm not sure the sponge was dry. I'm going to scoot it over near the radiator."

"I'll help. I came to tell you the word's being spread. Anyone who's interested is to take sleds and go to the hill about one."

"You going?"

"I plan to. Why? Did you think I wouldn't?"

"You can't tell about girls," Neal said. "When they're going to be too grown up for such fun."

"I'm not," Mary Anne said. "And in no hurry to be."

"That's fine with me," Neal said.

Mary Anne tried to think who she could call. *Not Patty. She wouldn't go anyway. And Clay's probably already seen the Pritchard twins. They live across Walnut from him. Who'd like to go? I know! Carmelita. But she doesn't have a telephone.*

She'd never been to the apartment above the grocery store where Carmelita's family lived. She'd heard that Mrs. Garzia didn't speak English and wouldn't come to the door when people knocked. *I could go and see if Lita's there,* she thought. Then she remembered what Carmelita said about working for Mrs. Lyons. So she hurried downstairs and looked up the number of the foster home. "Yes, she's here," a soft voice said. Mary Anne heard children's voices in the background.

"Hello. Speak loudly, please," Carmelita said.

"This is Mary Anne. Are you going to work all day?"

"I could. Why do you ask?"

Mary Anne told her why she'd called and said, "I'll wait here until one. If you decide to take time off we can go together."

"Well, I'll see," Carmelita said. "I've always wanted to go. *Gracias.*"

Hasn't anyone ever asked her? Mary Anne thought. *I know I never did. Didn't even think of it. And all these years she's wanted to go. I guess Oak Hill needed a Friendly Forum a long time ago. To break up cliques — and make people feel included. People right here in our little town.*

By lunchtime Mary Anne had changed her mind four times about what to wear. Her jumper would be warm because it was lined. But it wouldn't swirl when she twirled on the snow like her accordion pleated skirt. *Will Mama let me wear it? And my red coat. Did Clay notice it because he liked it or because it's bright?*

Carmelita hadn't shown up by one. Neal wanted to go on but Mary Anne coaxed him to wait ten minutes. After that she said, "Mama, if she comes here she won't walk over to the hill. She's too shy to walk into the group. I hate to leave."

"I can walk with her," Ellen said. "I know the way."

"But you don't like to slide down the hill," Neal said.

"I didn't say I wanted to do that. I just like to be nice to people. Okay?"

"Okay," Neal said.

17

Mary Anne and Neal followed the boot-trampled path which led from the edge of the road across half of the field and up the slope. Clay was waiting at the top. His cheeks were apple red and he was brushing snow from the sleeves of his plaid Pendleton jacket. "I took a spill," he said. "The traffic was a little heavy that last trip."

"Is it slick?" Neal asked.

"It's getting that way. Every run packs the wet snow and now that the sun's behind a cloud there may not be any thawing."

"Who are all these kids?" Mary Anne asked. "I don't recognize many."

"I think you'd know almost everyone," Clay said, "if they took off their scarves and knit helmets."

Mary Anne made a dozen trips up and down the hill. Sometimes she rode down with Neal but more often with Clay. By the tenth trip the wide path was icy slick. The snow had polished the sled runners shiny and each ride was a breathtaking swoop. There were no trees between the hill and the road. Mary Anne thought of *Ethan Frome*, the story in her literature book about how the lives of three people were twisted and warped by the crash of a sled into a tree.

By three o'clock the only danger was that one sled would swerve into another. The crowd grew larger as the purplish shadows crept across the slope. Carmelita came late in the afternoon. Mary Anne saw her wave to Ellen and come across the field. She met her halfway. "I thought you weren't going to make it."

"Well, there was so much to do. And I had to buy some boots."

"Come on up. We'll find a place for you on a sled. So you can hitch a slide."

Clay took Carmelita down a few times and then she rode with Neal. Her brown eyes had sparkling glints of gold in them. "It's like flying," she said. "Only your feet are close to the gound."

Clay suggested that they stop at the drugstore before going home. "I've burned up a bushel of calories."

"Well, maybe I shouldn't," Carmelita said.

"Come on," Mary Anne said. "It isn't late and you know you're as hungry as we are."

The tables were all filled so they sat on high counter stools while they ate hamburgers and drank cups of foamy hot chocolate. Neal left first. "Neither rain nor snow keeps this paper boy from running his *Star* route," he said.

Carmelita walked with Mary Anne and Clay back to the general store. "It's been so — *bueno*," she said. "Thanks for asking me."

"Well, you're welcome," Mary Anne answered. "But this is your town too. You're included."

A shadow seemed to come across Carmelita's face. "Maybe. Sometimes."

Clay didn't turn off at Walnut Street. He kept on walking with Mary Anne and they kept talking. When they came to the front gate she said, "I heard Neal telling you about the project, the relief map. If you want to see it, come on in. I think he's going to take it to school in a day or two."

The house was still. Mary Anne hurried to the kitchen and read the note which told her the reason. "Rhoda called. The snowplow's been down the Spring-vale road. We'll be back before six. Peel these potatoes — please."

Mary Anne wished she hadn't asked Clay to come in. All at once she felt shy. But it wasn't her nature to be impolite. So she said, "You can go on up to Neal's room. It's on the right at the end of the hall."

She hurried to get the paring knife and filled a bowl with cold water. A strip of brown peeling was curling from the fourth potato by the time Clay came downstairs. He didn't ask if he could stay, just pulled out a chair and sat down. "Neal's worked hard on that project, hasn't he?"

"Yes. For weeks. But I think the hardest part has been keeping Little Matt from stepping on it."

"Is that the farm where you lived?"

"Well, not exactly. That's south of Springvale. We lived north on another section of land, a mile or so away."

The refrigerator motor started with a click and ran with a pulsing hum. Mary Anne dropped a potato into the bowl and water splashed on her arm. "You're wondering why we don't live out there now, aren't you?"

"What are you? A mind reader? Or is your ESP working?"

"Neither," Mary Anne said. "I think it's a logical question. My father works there. We live here, twelve miles away. You may not believe it, but our family never talked about this until a few nights ago. None of us want to move, no matter why we're here."

"Do you know something," Clay said. "You're a remarkable person."

"Well, thank you," Mary Anne said, blushing. "Not only for the 'remarkable' but for calling me a person. So many times people say things like 'she's a great girl' or 'he's a fine boy.' They somehow seem to leave out something. Anyway, that's how I feel."

"That's what I mean," Clay said. "You think deeply. And talk sense. Of course I've not been around you a lot. But you never seem to have gone through some of those silly stages."

"Like being boy crazy?"

"For one, yes. I've dodged several girls while they were in that phase. And some who never outgrew it."

"I don't think I exactly skipped over those times," Mary Anne said. She'd finished the potatoes and had pulled out a chair on the other side of the table. "I think I was more or less lifted over them. By my mother. But also by Grandfather Kirk. Of course he influenced my mother's attitudes."

"How? Or can you explain?"

"Yes. I think so," Mary Anne said. "Grandfather thinks children are people, distinct individuals, from the time they're born. And that they know so much more than adults realize." She went on to say that

Matthew Kirk sees all of life as a process of education, with only part of it taking place in the classroom. That there isn't an hour or even a minute when a child isn't absorbing something.

"I've heard Grandfather say many times, 'The trouble is so many kids get scanty fare for their minds.' And he's said something else as often: 'Folks don't give kids credit. They talk to them as if they were babies, at least until they're old enough to talk back and a lot of times longer.' "

"Maybe this explains why everyone says Mr. Kirk was such a great teacher."

"Do they say that? Oh, I know some do. Have you heard this too?"

"Yes. Mainly from my mother," Clay said.

"Grandfather has a sense of humor that I love. He'll be all upset because people baby talk to children or because they don't stop to answer questions. Then he'll stop and chuckle and say, 'Their silliness and thoughtlessness is not so hard on the kids. But it sure does delay the growing-up process for papa and mama.' "

"I'll bet he explained lots of things to your mother."

"Yes. And to us. You know my mother and father were separated for two or three years?"

"Well, I knew he didn't live here for a while. But — it — how could you not know how long?"

"That's easy," Mary Anne said. "You see Mama made everything seem natural. There was no real break, at least as far as I know. Grandma Garland was sick a lot — in hospitals far away. Papa had to go with her. And that wasn't unusual. He was gone most of the time before then. Little Matt was on the way. We moved here so Grandfather could take care of us. That's how it seemed then. After Grandma died, Papa had more time. He began to visit us more often. And we went out to the farm and cooked and cleaned for him and my other grandfather. I didn't even realize that my parents were separated."

"But you do now. Did your mother — but that's prying."

"That's all right. I want to talk. I don't know why. I never have before. Anyway, I think I'm growing up and becoming more aware what Mama went through. Things she says, things I remember, the way I feel, and even what scares me go together like pieces of a puzzle."

"I know what you mean," Clay said. "History's my favorite subject. Always has been. Every year we go into it a little deeper. I see things more clearly. Like I thought for a long time that all the people who wrote the Constitution were interested in equal representation for everyone."

"Weren't they?"

"No. A few wanted to tip the scales, give more power to what they called the landed gentry, and have an aristocracy. But going back to what you were saying. What scares you, Mary Anne?"

Warmth crept over her face, and Mary Anne sorted and resorted her thoughts before she put any of them into spoken words. Should she say what would sound natural? That she worried about death, not just hers but of people she loved? Should she pretend that she'd only meant that she was afraid her home would break up again? That her mother wasn't truly happy? *But this is not what I meant,* she thought.

She clasped her hands on the table, looked straight at Clay and said, "I'm scared of dating."

She waited for an answer. Would he take this as a sign that she didn't want to have anything to do with him? Would he think she was in some way unnatural — freakish?

"Do you think you're the only high school senior who's scared of dating — or of the type of relationship that's popular now?"

"I don't know. I've never talked to anyone about it. Are there others?"

"There are several," Clay said. "Oh, some are shy. But others don't want to enter into the go-steady, one person possessing another kind of thing. I don't. I'd feel trapped."

Well, that's a relief, Mary Anne thought. *I don't have to keep running if everyone's not chasing me.* Aloud she said, "I don't like that either. But there's a deeper reason why I've pulled back. I don't think I'm as strong as Mama. I couldn't survive as much pain."

"Have you talked to her about this?" Clay asked.

"No. It's been on the tip of my tongue lots of times. And I think Mama senses how I feel. Maybe that's why I never bring the subject into the open. If she thought talking would help me she'd start the conversation."

Clay looked at his watch. "I'd better go or my mother will send the town marshal out looking for me. But this I must say. I knew you were scared about dating even if not why. And I've been holding back on asking you out."

"I knew that."

"Does all you've said mean you wouldn't go? Like if I blurted out, 'Mary Anne, will you go with me to the all-school mixer,' would you say no?"

Mary Anne smiled. "I'd probably say yes, because you used one certain word."

"What word? What was my magic word?"

"Person. Going places with someone who thinks of me as a person, as an individual, not just as a girl — with certain — dimensions — is a release. But there's one other thing." She told what Connie said about her first date. How it spoiled a good friendship. "I wouldn't want that to happen."

"Maybe this will help. I've already had that experience."

"How was it?"

"Terrible. I'm still trying to forget it. Now. I have to go. Thanks."

"The same to you."

Mary Anne felt like singing or dancing and she didn't know why. Clay was still a friend. *But that's enough for now. And for him too. He's not serious as the kids mean it. So I don't have to be scared to go with him. Not now anyway.*

18

It took the pale sun of early November three days to melt the blanket of snow which had drifted over parts of three counties in a little less than seven hours. A few patches stayed longer, in the shade of hedge fences, beneath the rose bushes, and between the clods in the garden. Susan Garland said the newly plowed earth looked like a giant molasses cookie. "We used to buy them from a square box and a sweet, white icing was splotched over the crinkly top."

The weather changed several times before Thanksgiving. A week of barely freezing temperatures was followed by two days of cold rain. Dirk and the children ate at Susan's father's house on the second evening of the rainy spell. Nancy had tried a new recipe and as she put it, "I want someone on hand in case Matthew smells this and decides he doesn't like it."

"Don't you taste things first, Grandfather?" Ellen asked.

"No need," Matthew Kirk said. "Smelling is the larger part of tasting."

The visit ended soon after Mary Anne and Nancy washed the dishes. "I promised Susan I'd get these kids to bed on time tonight," Dirk said. "They have a knack for coaxing me to let them stay up just a little longer, and even later than that."

"Children have been doing that for time immemorial," Matthew Kirk said.

"Grandfather, what's 'time immemorial'?" Ellen asked.

"Well, it means beyond memory. I don't ordinarily use such long words. But they're up there in the attic of my mind. Need to get them out and dust them off now and then."

Mr. Kirk followed the five-sixths of the Garland family out to the porch. "This is seesaw weather," he said. "Can't tell which way it's going to tip. A little colder and we'll have sleet. A bigger dip and it'll snow."

"Well, I hope it stays balanced until Susan gets home," Dirk said. "Good night, sir. You'd better get inside. This wet cold goes right to the bone."

Mary Anne walked with her father while the others ran on ahead, turning sideways so the rain wouldn't hit their faces. "Your grandpa," Dirk said. "I'd rather listen to him talk than anyone I ever heard on radio. He — well, he has a way with words."

"I know," Mary Anne said.

"I can see why people say he was a good teacher."

"That's plain to me too. He teaches every time he speaks."

Rain was still slashing the window when Mary Anne went to sleep, but the silver light of winter sunshine slanted across the floorboards the next morning. Some days were overcast and a few were fair before another snow fell. It came softly on Saturday morning and barely covered the ground.

Ellen came to waken Mary Anne that morning. "You'd better hurry if you're going to be ready to go to Grandpa's."

"It's not even daylight."

"It was until it began to snow."

Mary Anne swung her feet to the floor and walked to the window thinking, *If we're going to have a blizzard, I wish Ellen and I hadn't promised to stay all night with Grandpa Garland. I'd rather be snowed in here. But he's counting on us.*

A powdering of soft flakes filtered through the air but melted as soon as it settled on the walks, grass, and street. "I'll be down as soon as I dress," Mary Anne said. "Have you had your breakfast?"

"No. Because it's not cooked yet."

"But you said Papa was ready to leave."

"No. I didn't," Ellen said. "I said you'd better hurry if — "

"Okay. Okay. Scoot."

"You ladies figuring on staying a week?" Dirk Garland said as he looked at the luggage at the front door. Each had a suitcase. Mary Anne was taking a satchel of books and Ellen had stuffed a shopping bag with her Raggedy Ann doll, three coloring books, crayons in a baking powder can, and a new set of jacks. Susan came to the door with the two-handled basket she'd labeled "The commuter." It went back and forth between Oak Hill and Springvale carrying prepared foods one way and products of the farm the other.

"What's in there this time?" Mary Anne asked. "You didn't have to send meals. I can cook. That's part of why I'm going."

"I know," her mother said. "I'm sending mainly snacks. Chocolate-covered grahams and a few other things. And naturally I'll bring Sunday's dinner."

The day and evening passed quickly. Ellen went to the cornfield with her father and grandfather. She said she wanted to sit in the back corner of the wagon and watch ears of corn come from the picker spout. She came to the little barn to warm up while her father shoveled each load into the slatted crib.

Mary Anne swept, dusted, and scrubbed. *It doesn't really need it, though,* she thought. *Grandpa's so neat. But he doesn't use furniture polish much or Bon Ami on the windows.* She wandered outside when the sun came out an hour before noon, and followed the fencerow until she found a cluster of bittersweet vines. Frost had cracked the light orange berries and the new petals cupped a tangerine center. "I'll get some for Mama and put the rest in the brown pitcher on the mantel of the fireplace."

Connie Collins came to the door while they were eating potato pancakes, smoked sausage, and buttered cabbage. "Want more company?" she asked.

"Sure do," Seth Garland said. "There's enough bedroom for four up in the loft."

"Well, I can't stay all night," Connie said. "Just until evening. My dad's taking Aunt Rhoda and me to Dayton to visit another aunt."

The girls sat in front of the fireplace after the dishes were washed. They talked sometimes but were content to watch the flickering fingers of flame for minutes at a time.

Before Connie left she said, "You seem happier, more relaxed. Is there a special reason?"

"Well, yes, but not one exactly. A lot of things make life seem less painful, not so scary." For one thing, she wasn't letting Patty and Roger bother her anymore. "Those feelings have faded away. The Friendly Forum has helped. Meeting new kids made me realize there are lots of nice people in the world, that I don't have to depend on one for my security. And also that some have lived around the corner all the time."

"On Walnut Street?"

"How did you know — about Clay?"

"Oh! Anne. Anyone who looks at him when you're around can add things up without much mental strain."

Mary Anne's cheeks felt warm but she wasn't uncomfortable. She told Connie a part of the conversation she'd had with Clay the day after the snowstorm, but was interrupted when Mr. Collins came to the door.

"See you Monday," Connie said. "At the Forum meeting. Then Wednesday at the mixer. And every day after Thanksgiving — when the Springvale bus takes us to Oak Hill."

After Connie left, Mary Anne wished she had asked for a ride to the Christ's Chapel Church the next morning. It would be good to see whoever she still knew. And she didn't like to get in the habit of not going to church. *Of course I coax to stay at home sometimes. But Sunday never seems right when I get my way.*

Later when Mary Anne was slipping to sleep she remembered that Connie was going to Dayton. "That's why she didn't mention church. They wouldn't go that far just for an evening. They're staying overnight."

By noon the next day Mary Anne was ready to go home. She liked being at the farm and loved the look and feel of the little barn. But she kept wondering what was going on in Oak Hill. *Has anyone called? Or stopped by to see me?*

Her mother answered the first part of this question as she heated crusty chicken and sprinkled brown sugar over buttered sweet potatoes. "Clay called this morning."

"He did? Did he say why?"

"Yes. Some young people are getting together at his house to make decorations for the all-school party. At four. I told him we'd have you back in time."

After the meal Susan and Seth Garland yielded to Matt and Ellen's coaxing to go hickory nut hunting. Neal was given permission to ride Captain up and down the road, with the provision that he stop in the grass when cars approached. "He's a mite jumpy if someone races a motor," Seth said.

Mary Anne decided to finish her homework and leave the evening free for whatever might happen. She put a table-board across the arm of the easy chair and worked steadily for nearly an hour. The scratching of her pen, the hiss of burning logs, and the clicking of upward flying sparks were the only sounds until her father came in the door.

"I thought you'd changed your mind and gone to the woods."

"No," Dirk said. "I helped Neal get started. Then I refilled the mangers with hay."

Dirk went to the kitchen, then he walked first to one window then another before sitting down on the edge of his father's high-backed rocker.

"To tell the truth," he said, "I came in because I wanted to talk to you."

Mary Anne looked up and thought. *He looks uneasy.*

"Is something wrong, Papa? Have I done something?"

"No. No. Not you," Dirk said. "It's an old wrong I want to rectify." He smiled and rubbed his chin with one forefinger. "That's a word that's been in the attic of *my* mind a long time. I don't know as I *ever* made much use of it."

Mary Anne wished she could help her father. He seemed to be struggling. "I don't know how to get started," he said. "But this conversation was triggered when the Gilbert boy called this morning. Your Mama tell you?"

Mary Anne nodded.

"That was the signal. I knew it was time for me to tell you not to be afraid of life."

Mary Anne's eyes filled with tears. "You knew."

"Yes. I'm not as blind as I used to be. The look in your eyes the day we talked about the quail was like the look I used to glimpse in your mother's eyes — and ignore. The punishing part is knowing that I caused that pain." He pounded the arm of the rocking chair with a doubled fist.

He began to talk freely as if a pent-up pressure was being released. He said that Susan was the only girl he'd ever wanted to marry and that he'd been afraid she'd change her mind if she got to know him well. "It was a bad time for her to be making decisions. And I knew it. Her mama had died and her home wasn't the same. Maybe she jumped into marriage for security — which I never gave her."

"Why, Papa? If you loved her."

"I reckon a person can't give what he doesn't have. I was brought up thinking that money, work, and land could give whatever a person needs. That personal relationships came second. I didn't know any better until your mama took you back to Oak Hill."

"Do you think Mama was wrong to do that?"

"No. No. She did the only thing that had a chance of straightening us out. I guess you might say she retraced her steps to put her life on the right path. Not only for herself, but for you kids and, as it turned out, for me."

"I understand," Mary Anne said. "Partly anyway. Mama needs to be herself and she wants all of us to have the same right."

"I know. That's why I insisted she go back to school. She would've gone on if I hadn't taken advantage of her unsettled feelings and rushed her into getting married."

"I didn't know more education was your idea," Mary Anne said. "I thought Mama was going because she might want to teach when Matt's in school."

"Maybe she will. It's up to her. That shows how

much I've changed. There was a time when I'd have said the only good reason for spending good money to go to college is to make more money."

Dirk glanced at the clock on the mantel. The gold pendulum glinted in the firelight and the hands marked the hour of three. "I'd better cut this short if we're going to get you back by four. But there's something else. Another point. And this is what pains me most."

"Papa," Mary Anne said, "I don't want you to torture yourself because of me."

"Not *because* of you, Skeezicks, for you. It's like this. I've seen how you sort of drew into a shell after you got into high school. Your mama and I talked about this now and then. She said not to worry, that she was slow in growing up. And right then and there I suspected what you might be thinking."

"You did? Let's see if you're right."

"Well. You're so much like Susan. I see it. Everyone who knows both of you remarks about the resemblance. You were nearly twelve when you went to Oak Hill to live, and being so close to your mama you had to know something was wrong."

"Not really," Mary Anne said. "Not between you and Mama. Because things weren't too much different."

"Because I was gone a lot and didn't say much when I was around?"

Mary Anne nodded. "But I did notice something, a sad look in Mama's eyes. I didn't think much about it then. Probably because she tried to protect us."

Mary Anne began to be afraid that someone would come in before she finished what she knew she had to say. It was time, the right moment.

"This is why I've sort of hidden from life, Papa. Growing up means becoming aware of sadness. And since Mama and I *are* alike in so many ways I've wondered what would happen if I —"

"If you were unhappy in marriage?"

"Yes. I don't want to hurt *you*. But I know now that she was. That things were hard sometimes."

"Most of the time," Dirk said. "Until — well, there's no time to go into that."

"I don't think we need to," Mary Anne said. "I know Mama's happy now. I'd know that even if she hadn't told me."

At this moment it was Dirk Garland's eyes that glistened with tears. After a dozen or more pats of his left foot, he went on. "I want you not to be so scared of growing up, Mary Anne. Remember this. You may be sensitive and have pained feelings like Susan. But you also have her strength. And besides that, there's no rush about going out with boys. The hickory tree leafs out a lot later in the spring than the others. I never did hear anyone make fun of a hickory because it budded late. Or build a fire under it to speed up things. Take your time, Skeezicks. Be free to grow up your way."

"Thank you, Papa. Thank you for loving me enough to put yourself through so much pain."

Dirk smiled. "I guess you could say that word *rectify* got a good dusting this afternoon — a long overdue polish."

The Author

Dorothy Hamilton was born in Delaware County, Indiana, where she still lives. She received her elementary and secondary education in the schools of Cowan and Muncie, Indiana. She attended Ball State University, Muncie, and has taken work by correspondence from Indiana University, Bloomington, Indiana. She has attended professional writing courses, first as a student and later as an instructor.

Mrs. Hamilton grew up in the Methodist Church and participated in numerous school, community, and church activities until the youngest of her seven children was married.

Then she sensed that the Lord was leading her to become a private tutor. This service has become a mission of love. Several hundred girls and boys have come to Mrs. Hamilton for gentle encouragement, for renewal of self-esteem, and to learn to work.

The experiences of motherhood and tutoring have inspired Mrs. Hamilton in much of her writing.

Seven of her short stories have appeared in quarterlies and one was nominated for the American Literary Anthology. Since 1967 she has had fifty serials published, more than four dozen short stories, and several articles in religious magazines. She has also written for radio and newspapers.

Mrs. Hamilton is author of a growing shelf of books: *Anita's Choice, Christmas for Holly, Charco, The Killdeer, Tony Savala, Jim Musco, Settled Furrows, Kerry, The Blue Caboose,* and *Mindy.*